Dear Brio Girl,

Just like Jacob in the book of Genesis, Jacie finds herself wrestling with God . . . that is, if God even exists. She tries to ignore the questions reeling inside her head and throws herself into any activity she can find. But those questions, her impending graduation, and other changes make Jacie feel like her world will never be all right again.

Jacie's friends, especially Tyler, are worried about this wrestling match that never seems to end. But she is tired of church answers and easy outs; she's ready for something that's tangible and real. Are you ready for that too? Then hold on tight. I'm excited to see if Jacie's story will affect your life the way it did mine.

Your friend,

Susie Shellenberger, BRIO Editor
www.briomag.com

BRIO GIRLS®

from Focus on the Family®
and
Tyndale House Publishers, Inc.

---

1. *Stuck in the Sky*
2. *Fast Forward to Normal*
3. *Opportunity Knocks Twice*
4. *Double Exposure*
5. *Good-bye to All That*
6. *Grasping at Moonbeams*
7. *Croutons for Breakfast*
8. *No Lifeguard on Duty*
9. *Dragonfly on My Shoulder*
10. *Going Crazy Till Wednesday*
11. *When Stars Fall*
12. *Bad Girl Days*

brio® girls

REAL Faith MEETS REAL Life℠

Hannah Tyler Becca Solana

Bad Girl Days

Created and Written by

LISSA HALLS JOHNSON

TYNDALE

Tyndale House Publishers, Inc.
Wheaton, Illinois

Bad Girl Days
by Lissa Halls Johnson

A Focus on the Family Book Published by Tyndale House Publishers, Wheaton, Illinois 60189

Focus on the Family books are available at special quantity discounts when purchased in bulk by corporations, organizations, churches, or groups. Special imprints, messages, and excerpts can be produced to meet your needs. For more information, contact: Focus on the Family, 8605 Explorer Drive, Colorado Springs, CO 80920; phone (800) 932-9123.

Library of Congress Cataloging-in-Publication Data
Johnson, Lissa Halls, 1955-
Bad girl days / created [and] written by Lissa Halls Johnson.
p. cm. — (Brio girls (Tyndale House Publishers))
"Focus on the family."
Summary: Still shaken by Dinah's death and distrusting God, Jacie desperately attempts to fill the void in her life and cope with the looming changes that high school graduation promises, while her friends try to help her regain her faith.
ISBN 1-58997-091-8
[1. Trust in God—Fiction. 2. Faith—Fiction. 3. High schools—Fiction. 4. Schools—Fiction. 5. Self-esteem—Fiction. 6. Christian life—Fiction.] I. Title. II. Series.

PZ7.J63253Bad 2005
[Fic]—dc22 2004021637

Editor: Mick Silva
Cover design by Lookout Design Group, Inc.

Printed in the United States of America

For my mom,
who taught me to hold on to God even when there seemed
to be evidence that He had abandoned me; to trust,
even when there seemed to be evidence He was untrustworthy;
and that honest questions asked of God draw us
closer to Him whether we receive an answer or not.

• • •

With special thanks to my daughter,
Misty Johnson,
whose graduation speech was used for this book.

LISSA HALLS JOHNSON is on staff at Focus on the Family where she writes some books, edits others, and torments her co-workers with outrageous questions, flying toys, and generally being a nuisance. When she's not held captive by her gray cubicle, she's hanging out at the foot of the mountains she adores, usually hiking, skiing, or snowshoeing with her husband, Rich and dog, Kyna. Previously a member of the ADVENTURES IN ODYSSEY® creative team, she's completely surprised that she's the author of 16 novels for teens and the young reader.

chapter 1

Jacie fingered the material of her graduation gown. It slipped through her fingers, cool to the touch. She'd felt satin many times before. But now, sewn into this shape, it had a sense of power behind it. There was a fear. A fullness. Anticipation. An ending. A beginning. *Freedom*.

She wasn't sure she wanted the freedom. She liked the safety of Stony Brook High. She knew the school's world, the society, the way people connected—or didn't. It surrounded her in safety. She might as well have been sitting in a well-manned police station. She knew her role at Stony Brook. She didn't know what each day would bring, but it was always a variation on the same theme.

What would life be like out in the "real" world? From what she'd seen through her mother, it was hard, painful, lonely, and exhausting. There seemed to be a lot of empty striving. Reaching for things that didn't happen. A lot of pointless trudging to work, then home again. The same household chores popping up and demanding attention week after week. There was the momentary fun event with friends for distraction. But then it was back to the endless routine.

Jacie lifted the mortarboard and placed it on her curls. She moved the pointed cap about, trying to find the place where it set the best, where it looked the best. But no matter where she placed it, it didn't give her what she needed the most—wisdom about the future. Direction. She was still afraid. Still looking at a blank screen or one of those posters that looks like swirls and designs, but in reality has a picture in it if you look at it just right. As hard as she looked at her future, she couldn't see the picture.

She took the graduation gown and held it up to herself. The one-size-fits-all gown hung to her ankles. Good thing she was short. But *black*? Why black? To signal the doom of what lay ahead of them? Death too young?

Like Dinah.

Jacie threw the cap onto her unmade bed.

"They're here!" her mom's voice called.

Jacie threw open her bedroom door. "Come on up!"

Footsteps pounded up the stairs, voices floating ahead of them. "Shall we tell her now?"

"Shhh."

"I'm *not* going to shush. It's a free country."

Jacie's grin started from deep inside where her friends had become intertwined with her soul. What would she do without them?

And then it struck her. They would scatter next fall, like leaves blown upon the wind. And then the winter of her heart would move in.

"What a mess!" Solana said as she burst into the room.

"Big deal," Hannah said, flopping onto the end of the bed.

She picked up the mortarboard and put it over her face. "Maybe we should wear them like this," her muffled voice said.

Becca flopped onto the other end of the bed. "Might as well. In a class of 360 or whatever it is, you're pretty anonymous anyway."

"Not Jacie," Hannah said, lifting the cap from her face and sitting up.

Jacie dropped to the floor, grabbing Alex, her huge floppy stuffed bunny. She wrapped her arms around him. "Don't remind me," she groaned. "Whatever possessed me—"

Solana helped herself to a stick of grape licorice from a bag lying on Jacie's makeshift desk. "Probably the spirit of Darg who gets grads to do all kinds of weird things. Hence, Darg—'grad' spelled backwards."

"I can't talk to anyone without getting tongue-tied and—"

"We don't want to hear about it," Becca said, inspecting the pile of clothes scattered on the bed. "This is cute. New?"

"Goodwill."

"We need to go shopping again," Hannah said, holding up a darling skirt.

"Why don't you want to hear about it?" Jacie asked. "You're supposed to be my friends."

"We are," Solana said. "But—"

"Everyone's going to love you," Hannah said.

"You can't say that," Jacie said. "You don't know."

"They already love you," Solana said.

Jacie snorted. "Yeah, right."

"You are *the* most friendly person in the entire world," Hannah said. "Bar none."

"Read the *Stony Brook High Times*," Becca said. "Clear as truth. Right there." She jumped up from the floor and rummaged through the papers on the desk, pulling out the latest issue.

"Great photo of the elusive Morton the Moose, by the

way," Solana said to Hannah, toasting her with the licorice. "He looks fabulous with the golden red of the rocks behind him."

"Thanks. Took me a week of darting in and out of the Glen Eyrie Conference Center grounds. I felt like a spy or something."

"See?" Becca said, opening up the newspaper. She had also taken a piece of licorice. She tapped the paper with it. "Right here. 'Senior Will and Testaments': 'Jacie Noland leaves to win the nicest person in the world award. She leaves to spread sunshine everywhere she goes.' "

"Oh," Jacie said sarcastically, yanking the paper from Becca's hands and tossing it back on the desk. "You expect me to believe anything you guys say?"

"I didn't write it," Solana said, sounding bored. "Why would I?"

"Wasn't me," Hannah said. "Too busy trying to capture Morton for the picture."

Becca shrugged. "I forgot. I was going to write Solana's, but someone else beat me to it."

"Tyler then—"

"Cut mine out and make a poster," Solana said dryly. "I think I can say it by heart—'Solana Luz leaves to sass her way through UC Berkeley's science department, leaving a trail of brokenhearted boys falling behind her.' "

"Face it, Jacie," Becca said. "One of your adoring fans wrote it."

Jacie's face lit up and her heart warmed. *Damien!*

Solana shook her head. "Not Damien. I asked."

Jacie's mind fought to find other options, but came up with nothing.

"Fact is, Jacie, almost everyone in this school knows you."

"And likes you," Solana added. "Most people know me, but 90 percent of them don't like me."

"And the other 10 percent are guys," Hannah said.

"Hannah!" Becca said. "I can't believe you just said that."

"Believe it," Hannah said.

"I can't do it!" Jacie wailed. "I don't know why in the world—"

Hannah slid off the bed and hugged Jacie and the floppy bunny. "I know you're scared. I'd probably wet my pants if I were you."

Becca and Solana sat with their mouths gaping.

"What?" Solana asked. "No verse?"

"Wet your pants?"

Hannah looked at them, stroking Jacie's curls. "Sometimes the best answer is no answer." She looked at Jacie's wide eyes. "Truth is, I *would* be scared. Sometimes no verse will take away that kind of fear."

Jacie couldn't believe what Holy Hannah was saying. In the few short months since Hannah's Aunt Dinah's death in the train accident, they hadn't seen much of her. She'd been hiding out at home helping her mother care for the family while everyone grieved. Out-of-town family had come to stay for the local services. Hannah had cried and yelled more than Jacie had ever seen anyone do. The event had sliced Hannah's faith to nothing. She had fluctuated from peace to anger, questions to doubt, then back to the certainty of God's faithfulness again. Even now, she was barely holding it together. They all knew it. They could see it in her eyes.

"Thanks," Jacie told her.

"You'll do fine," Becca said. "Really you will. We wouldn't lie to you about that."

"If you need help—"

"Thanks, Sol. I do need your help."

"What can we do?" Hannah asked, leaning against the bed. She unfastened her hair, which fell around her in blonde waves.

"Let me practice the speech on you. And I want you to be totally honest."

Solana raised an eyebrow. "Really? You want me to be totally honest?" She wiggled the raised brow.

Jacie smiled. "Yes, Sol. I want you to be honest. I don't want to look like a fool in front of the entire graduating class and all the parents and all the sib—" Her voice drifted off as she could see the crowds of people in the World Arena all staring at her.

"And all the grandparents, friends, school supervisors, newscasters, and . . ."

"Stop it!" Hannah said to Solana, laughing for the first time that Jacie could remember since before the tragedy.

"You are *so* mean, Solana Luz," Jacie said. She stuck her tongue out at her.

"So!" Becca said, leaning against the door. "Practice."

"I'm not ready yet," Jacie said.

"Why not? You already did it in front of the faculty."

"I've got lots of things to do to change it and make it real."

"Like?" Hannah asked.

Jacie took a deep breath. "I don't really know for sure but I'm thinking about creating a painting and how our lives are a painting and that we are the artists and I'm thinking about actually taking an unfinished painting and maybe even a finished one and maybe even do a little painting on stage but I don't think I can do that but I thought that might be really good to have some sort of a visual if I could paint while I talked or something."

The three girls sat, looking at Jacie.

"What?"

"Are you done?" Solana asked. "Because I didn't want to jump in the path of that runaway train. Those words could have killed me."

Becca drew a sharp breath. "Sol!"

"Oh, Hannah." Solana slapped her hand over her mouth.

Hannah shook her head, tears in her eyes. "It's okay. It was funny. Really."

"I think that's a great idea, Jace," Becca said, reaching for another piece of licorice and offering the bag to the others. They all took one, chewing like a bunch of pensive cows.

"You think?"

"Yeah."

"The painting?"

"Let's see what you come up with first."

"The idea is awesome," Hannah said. "Perfect."

Their eyes locked. And Jacie knew. It *was* perfect.

"Here's another one!" Jacie's mom called up the stairway.

"Come on up, Tyler," Solana said, sticking her head out the door.

"How'd you know it was me?" Tyler asked, taking the steps two at a time as he always did.

"Everyone else is here."

"Except Nate!" Becca trilled about her boyfriend.

Tyler's face appeared in the door. "Great. Just what I was hoping for."

"Why are you all dressed up?" Hannah asked. "Have I ever seen you in a real dress shirt?"

At your aunt's funeral, Hannah, Jacie thought.

Tyler opened his mouth, and his eyes locked for a brief moment with Jacie's. She quickly looked away. He cleared his throat, put on a fake smile, and said, "I guess not."

"So what's the occasion?" Becca asked.

"I'll tell you in a minute," Tyler said, looking like he would explode if he didn't say something. But he turned Jacie's desk chair around and sat in it backward, straddling the seat and crossing his arms across the back.

"Are you sure?" Solana asked. "Because it looks like you're ready to pop a monkey if you don't."

Tyler just tapped his foot on the floor. "Oh, no."

"When do you plan on telling us?" Jacie asked, a look passing between them. It took her off guard. *What was that?*

"It depends." He threw a glance in Becca's direction.

No one said anything. Jacie played with the stuffed bunny's ear, feeling suddenly shy about Tyler being in the room. Hannah leaned against the bed, tracing sunlight patterns on the floor. Solana flipped through the school newspaper. Becca picked at the carpet. She sighed.

"Well, I have something to tell," Becca said. She continued to pick. She ran her fingers through the low shag, making designs in the pile. A fat tear dropped into the pattern.

"Becca?" Jacie asked.

Her voice choked. "Nate's moving."

chapter 2

All eyes turned to her. There was a stunned moment of thick silence.

Except for Tyler, who nodded.

Becca looked at him, tears pouring down her face. "You knew?"

"Yeah. He called me this morning."

The group surrounded Becca, holding her while she cried.

Tyler took Jacie's hand and squeezed it. Startled, Jacie looked at his other hand, which lay flat against Solana's. She felt her gaze drawn to him. He smiled at her and squeezed her hand again.

Jacie wanted to pour her love and sadness into Becca. But Tyler's hand distracted her.

Tyler tugged her hand until Jacie looked at him again. He jerked his head toward the door, let go of her hand, and tiptoed out.

Becca slowed her sobs to explain. "His dad's job is moving them next week to *Australia*! I guess there's some sort of urgent need. The company is buying their house and helping them move. They're even buying them a house down there."

"Wow, that's fast," Hannah said.

"Why not stay here until graduation?" Jacie asked.

"They don't believe in splitting up the family even for a few months."

"Good for them," Hannah said. "Not so good for you."

Becca wiped at her tears as if she were mad at them. "But shouldn't I just be happy for him and the fact that they are following God's will?"

"Who says God's will always makes us happy?" Hannah snapped.

"You, for one," Solana said. "Or is your memory gone?"

"Maybe yours is, Solana," Hannah said sharply. "Yeah, I used to say something like that. But I'm learning, okay? I guess God is too big for us to always understand His will. I, for one, certainly don't like it right now. And I bet Becca doesn't, either. We have to get to the point where we trust His will whether we like it or not."

"Do you?" Solana asked.

Hannah's eyes flashed. "Right now? No." She turned to Becca. "Do you trust God's will right now?"

Becca looked at her, a tear escaping to roll down her cheek. She swiped at it. Looked at Solana. Then Jacie. Then back at Hannah. "Not really."

Hannah reached over and gave Becca's hand a squeeze. A look of understanding passed between them.

You'd think we're starting a cheesy support group with all the hand squeezing going on here, Jacie thought.

Becca looked around. "Where'd Tyler go?"

Jacie bit her lip.

Solana shrugged. "He up and left in the middle of our hug fest."

"I'm right here," his voice said from the other side of the door.

"Get in here, you dork," Solana said.

"I can't."

"What are you *doing*?" Jacie asked.

"Come open the door."

"What? Your arm's broke?" Solana asked.

"Just come open the door. All of you."

The girls looked at each other and started to giggle. "He is *so* weird," Solana said as she walked on her knees toward the door. The other girls gathered around her. "Okay. Here goes," Solana said. She threw open the door.

Tyler was kneeling on the floor, a bouquet of red roses in his arms.

Jacie had no idea what anyone else was doing, but she was quite aware that she was holding her breath.

Tyler cleared his throat and said, "Will you go to the prom with me?"

No one said anything.

Tyler gave each girl a rose from the beautiful bouquet. "I would be delighted if you would go to the prom with me."

"Which one of us?" Becca whispered.

"All of you," Tyler said, his voice soft and full of emotion.

"But—" Becca started to say.

"I know," Tyler said. "The senior prom is supposed to be one guy asking one special girl to be with him for the evening. But I can't imagine choosing any other girl from the entire school. None of them mean as much to me as you four do. And so this guy is asking his four best girls to be with him for the evening."

Jacie felt a smile begin somewhere inside and spread across her face. "I'd love to, Tyler Jennings."

There. That look from him again.

"You're not Ramón," Solana said. "But you'll do."

"I'll take that as a compliment," Tyler said. "Even if you didn't mean it that way."

"I didn't," Solana teased.

"Wow," Becca said, tears still running down her cheeks. "With Nate moving I figured—"

"I asked his permission," Tyler said, smiling at her. Then he turned to Hannah. "I know there's someone you'd rather go with."

Only after Dinah's death did Hannah discover that her secret admirer of nearly a year was Grant, the coffee guy at Copperchino's. He had revealed his intentions to court Hannah in the future. Since then, they didn't seek each other out, but talked warmly whenever the gang went for coffee, or when she ran into him at school.

Hannah rolled her eyes. "As if. Grant and I won't date. We'll only court—if it ever comes to that."

"So?" Tyler asked. "Will you go with us?"

"If my parents say yes," Hannah said, stifling a giggle.

"What's so funny?" Tyler asked.

"Imagine. My first and probably only date of my entire life, and I'm going with three girls and a wannabe rock star."

• • •

Jacie played with her stack of 3 x 5 cards. On them were words she'd written, then presented to a few members of the faculty. Eight other students had also tried out. But the faculty had chosen Jacie.

Good morning, seniors! Can you believe it?
We're finally here! Today is the first day
of a new beginning.

In two short months, she would stand in front of over a thousand people in the World Arena in Colorado Springs and present the graduation speech. When the announcement that she had been chosen was read over the loudspeaker during second period, Jacie could hardly believe it. For one entire day, she walked without her feet touching the ground. Everything looked beautiful. Even the bare trees, stark lines etched against a brilliant blue sky, took on new beauty.

Alexander Graham Bell once said, "When one door closes, another opens. But we often look so regretfully upon the closed door, we are unable to see the one that has opened for us."

As we, Stony Brook High's graduating class, embark on a new journey, let us not forget all that we leave behind, but also, let us not fail to grasp the newness of what lies ahead. Next year we will be taking many different paths, away from what we have always known. Along the way, we will meet new people, make new friends, go new places, and learn new things about the world and about ourselves. The transition from here to there may not be easy, but it will present many opportunities for growth and change. If we do not embrace these opportunities to change and grow stronger, we might as well have never moved at all.

The next day she crashed. "What have I done?" she begged of her friends. They all laughed at her, reminding her of the times she'd given speeches in elementary school competitions—and won.

"You'll do fine," Becca said without a hint of sympathy for her terror. "You're always like this. And then you get in front of a crowd and shine."

Solana rolled her eyes. "The day you do something poorly, let me know, Miss Gifted-At-Everything."

"Like talking about my faith?" Jacie reminded her.

"As if I care about that."

We can't stay where we are and do well. We must go forward, work hard, and accept changes. Often, that which we never expected becomes far greater and better than what we could ever imagine.

But when she wrote those words she hadn't known God would snuff out Hannah's Aunt Dinah and her unborn baby in a random accident. Before Aunt Dinah's death, she'd written the words with confidence.

Now she didn't know what she would do. What would she say to her fellow classmates? That there was no hope for the future? That God could randomly destroy them with horrible events that change everything—forever?

Before Nate's moving, before Aunt Dinah's train car plunging from a bridge in Africa, before Becca's burning down the Community Center and trashing her knee, before Tyler's being rejected from his only choice of colleges. Before all these things, she trusted God with her future.

But now? Now she couldn't trust anything.

A sudden memory flashed in her mind. At the beach, five years old. Falling sand suddenly caving in. Surrounded, trapped in the hole she'd been digging. It came in so fast, she couldn't get out. Just before it reached her open mouth, her father reached in and grabbed her under her arms and yanked her out. Her future felt like that now. The safe place she'd thought she'd dug was caving in on her.

chapter 3

"Boy, are you ever in trouble," Becca said at Jacie's front door.

"Hello to you, too," Jacie said. "Come on in."

"No time, really. Just had to come let you know. Gotta run!" Becca turned and trotted stiff-legged down the townhouse stairs. She'd recently gotten her brace off and still couldn't move like she used to.

Jacie shook her head and held back a laugh. "Becca," she called.

Without turning around, Becca waved her hand. "No time. Lots to do for Nate's going away party."

"BECCA!"

Becca stopped, and stretched out her hands. "WHAT?" she asked, exasperated.

"You came all this way just to tell me I'm in trouble? With who? Why?"

Becca stared, blank. "I didn't tell you?"

Jacie put her hands on her hips and tilted her head, saying nothing.

Becca slapped her hand over her mouth. "I didn't, did I?" she said, the words muffled. She dropped her hand. "Mrs. Robeson wants to talk with you."

"When?"

"Probably yesterday. But since you already blew that, I guess as soon as you can get there."

"What did I do?"

Becca shrugged. "How should I know? She never tells me anything." She turned, waving over her shoulder. "See ya!"

Jacie informed her mom of her errand, grabbed her keys and mini-purse, and trotted down the stairs to their carport. She opened the door of her Tercel—which had recently developed an agonizing creak—and slipped inside. She stopped a moment to take a deep breath before plugging the key into the ignition. She turned the engine, punched the radio buttons until a station with a good song rang into the car, and shifted into reverse.

"What did I do now?" she spoke aloud while looking over her shoulder. The words came from her mouth a split second before the rear tires raised the car up and down, and a definite crunch punctured the old Smashing Pumpkins' song. "How appropriate," Jacie said, shifting into neutral and pulling on the parking brake. She opened the reluctant squeaky door and dropped to her knees, peering underneath.

"Great. Just great." She reached under and retrieved a crushed plastic toy with large, round black ears and a red coat. "Little Bunny Foo-Foo" began to play in her head while Smashing Pumpkins played in the background. Why that song, she wasn't sure. Perhaps because the toy looked an awful lot like a large plastic mouse that had received more than a bop on the head.

As if that weren't enough noise, a very short person ran up next to her and shrieked. "LOOK WHAT YOU DID TO MY MICKEY! YOU BROKE MY MICKEY MOUSE! I'LL NEVER HAVE ANOTHER ONE! I'M TELLING MOM! THAT WAS MY FAVORITE TOY!"

Jacie opened her mouth to apologize, but the shrieks didn't stop. Forced wails shot out of the short person in a phony torrent as she turned and ran into the townhouse with the blue door.

Jacie took the ruined toy to the blue door. She knocked, but she knew there was no way anyone with normal hearing could distinguish her knock with that horrible shrieking and wailing going on inside. She was tempted to just drop the crushed pieces onto the doormat and walk away. And then she hated herself for her callous response. A kid's whole life could be wrapped up in one special toy.

She rang the doorbell.

The shrieks moved away. A door slammed. The shrieks were muffled by distance and wood. A round face appeared at the opening door. "Yes?"

"I'm so sorry," Jacie said, holding out the broken Mickey. "I didn't see it. I'll replace it."

The woman paused. She looked beyond Jacie, then stepped into view. Her tattered bathrobe was pulled around her stocky frame. "Thanks." She closed her eyes and shook her head. "I call her Noisy Nora, after the book. She can work up a tizzy about anything and everything."

"I'll replace it," Jacie said.

The woman shook her head. "Nora doesn't take care of her things. She didn't even like this toy until you ran over it. So forget it. She needs to learn to be more responsible." She stopped and gave a quick jerk of her head back toward the depths of the house. "Listen. She's not even crying anymore. No audience—

no point in tears. I simply don't know what to do with that kid. I'd even bet she put that toy there hoping for someone to run over it. Drama, drama, drama. That kid lives for it."

Jacie was kind of mesmerized by the whole thing.

"Camerin," the woman said sticking out her hand.

"Jacie," she responded, putting her hand in Camerin's. "I live upstairs and over two. 3113. Are you sure I can't replace the Mickey Mouse?"

Camerin put her hand up. "No. Nora has enough toys. Her father spoils her silly. And his parents are filthy rich. They seem to think a child can't go a month without new toys. Nora will forget about Mickey by tonight. If she doesn't, I'll let you know."

"All right. I'm awfully sorry."

Camerin flashed a smile and Jacie turned and walked to her car. This time she checked all around, finding three more items in the parking lot. She placed them at the blue door, then continued on her errand.

The Community Center's temporary office sat in a squat building on Fourth Street. Jacie felt her insides quivering as she opened the glass-paneled door. Angela the receptionist sat behind a low metal desk. "Why, Jacie! I had no idea you were coming in. Your name isn't on the roster."

"I guess Mrs. Robeson wants to see me."

Angela raised an eyebrow. She leaned forward and said in a loud whisper, "At least she's in a good mood today. The builders are coming along well in rebuilding the center. No setbacks." She winked. "She probably won't eat you this time."

Angela picked up the phone, punched in some numbers, and announced Jacie's arrival.

Jacie smiled, her nerves steadied. Really, Mrs. R wasn't so bad. She could be intimidating, and if you did something wrong you'd certainly hear about it. But truly, she was more businesslike than anything else. No one had died in her presence—even Becca, who had inadvertently burned down much of the Community Center.

"Go on in," Angela said, hanging up the phone.

Jacie rapped a couple times on the office door, then let herself in. "Good afternoon, Mrs. Robeson."

"Hello, Jacie," Mrs. R said, smiling her usual restrained smile. "Have a seat."

Jacie sat on the edge of the cracked plastic-upholstered chair.

"I would like you to teach an art class here at the center."

Jacie felt two things at once. Her heart leapt for joy while her stomach turned cartwheels of nerves. "Are you sure?"

Mrs. R's smile softened. "Of course I'm sure. What I'm not sure of is who will come. I'd like to limit it to the children, but adults might show up as well. Would that be a problem?"

Jacie shook her head. Of course it would be a problem. She didn't want to teach adults. She really didn't want to teach children. She didn't know how to teach. What to teach. If she *could* teach. She didn't know if she had the time. She didn't want to have the time.

"Can we start next Thursday?"

Jacie opened her mouth to answer, feeling a bit like someone who'd forgotten how to speak. Kind of like her grandmother, who did that a lot right before she died. She'd nod at what someone said and open her mouth. Her jaw would move up and down a few times, her eyes would grow wide as if startled, and her mouth would clamp shut.

Jacie cleared her throat, hoping that would jar some words out. "I guess."

"Will you need any supplies?"

At that, Jacie's mind unlocked. "Lots of paper. The bigger the better. Small paper, too, for those who think big is intimidating. Cheap poster paints actually work well for children.

The bright colors are inviting. Black is good, too, for those who need it. Anything else you might throw away, give to me and I could probably find use for it—bubble wrap, packing peanuts, old macaroni, smooth rocks, sticks, even colored paper that has printing on half of it. Scissors, glue, clay, or Play-Doh. Whatever you think is trash, send it my way and let me decide."

Mrs. R nodded as if she'd just been given a supply list from the construction workers. "I'll watch for building materials as well."

"Nothing sharp," Jacie said, then regretted it. Mrs. R wasn't stupid.

"Next Thursday at 4:00."

"Thursday at 4:00."

Jacie stood, knowing Mrs. R never had time nor inclination for chitchat. She shook Mrs. R's hand, feeling quite grown up.

She smiled at Angela on her way out. "I'll see you next Thursday." She leaned over the desk and whispered, "I'm going to be teaching an art class!"

Angela nodded once and reached for her volunteer clipboard. "I'll put you down."

Jacie slipped into the car, joy and fear dancing together in her heart. Working with little kids, teaching them about art. What could be better than that?

So why are my hands shaking?

This will be FUN, she told herself. *Something to take my mind off everything else in my life for at least once every week.*

She'd have to go to Raggs by Razz and let them know she needed Thursday afternoons off. At least her boss liked the employees to do volunteer work. How many times had Mrs. Gumphrey told them at staff meetings to find a place to volunteer?

She cranked up the radio and sang at full volume to an overplayed tune. She tried to focus on the lyrics to drown out the fear. But it was louder than her radio.

You? Teach art?

She could see herself standing in front of a group of wide-eyed, curious people. And them all looking to her to be the expert. The one in the know. They would all look at her, eager to become great artists. But what, really, did she know about being a great artist? She only knew how to be an artist who sometimes puts out work that some very cloistered people like. If her work were to go national, she knew very well what the reaction would be.

"Awkward."

"Hopelessly juvenile."

"Pedantic."

Her heart started to flap inside her chest. Her legs started to tremble.

She wasn't an expert. She fumbled along through her own art, stumbling, trying new things that didn't work. Producing pieces that were way below anyone's standards. She looked on very few pieces with pride. Mostly she was a beginner. A foolish, bumbling beginner.

What was she thinking? What was Mrs. R thinking? Had she ever seen any of Jacie's pathetic work?

She sighed. Mrs. R had seen plenty of her work. Becca and Hannah had seen to that. Maybe that's why Becca had been coming to Jacie's shack so often lately, asking a million questions as she flipped through the pages of Jacie's portfolio.

So why had Mrs. R wanted her anyway?

Ahhh . . . Mrs. R must be uneducated in art.

Jacie wondered if she should tell her. If she should let Mrs. R know that she recruited a teacher who doesn't really know what she is doing. But then, Mrs. R, as gruff as she can be, chooses whoever she can get to volunteer. And perhaps she tried other sources for art teachers, couldn't find anyone else, and was settling for Jacie.

Jacie downshifted into second, then braked to stop. She could hear her driving instructor's voice in her head, telling her to count to three, look left, right, left, then proceed when safe.

Was she safe? Jacie wondered as she accelerated through the empty intersection. Was some train going to fall off a bridge with her in it?

She turned the corner, bumped over the driveway, threw the car into park, and stared at the house.

Why am I here?

chapter 4

From the safety of her car, Jacie stared at the wreath on the front door. A winter wreath. Not really Christmas. Winter. She took the keys from the ignition and fiddled with them, wondering if she should go up there to the big door between the potted plants that didn't die in winter. She didn't know what they were called. But they lived on.

She'd always felt at home here. She'd felt at home at all her friends' homes for lots of years now. So why this funny feeling?

You dummy. Just go home.

The garage door creaked and began to move upward.

"Jacie!" Mrs. Jennings said, coming toward her car.

Jacie opened the door. "Hi, Mrs. Jennings."

"Tyler's upstairs. You can yell at him or have Tyra go drag him out. He might have his headphones on. I need to get to the store. I totally forgot we have company coming tonight."

Jacie paused, halfway out of the car. "Oh, I'm sorry. I didn't know—"

Mrs. Jennings rolled her eyes and shook her head. "Jacie, it's never inconvenient to have you here. Tyler will be glad to see you." She gave Jacie a smile and got into her car.

Jacie walked through the garage and into the bright, country-decorated kitchen. Tyler was just walking in through another door. His face lit up. "Jace!"

"Hi." Jacie smiled. "I've . . . got some news. Thought I'd drop by to talk about it."

Tyler took a couple of running steps and slid across the wood floor on sock-covered feet. He yanked open the refrigerator and disappeared inside. He reappeared with a Dr Pepper and an orange soda. Popping open her drink first, he handed it to her. "Sorry. No orange juice." He jerked his head toward the family room.

He flopped on one end of the love seat. Jacie curled up on the other, feeling at once comfortable and uncertain.

"How embarrassed should I be about my art?" Jacie asked him, studying the top of her soda can. Lately she found it difficult to look into his expressive, deep blue eyes.

"Interesting way to put it. I'd say, *very*. Extremely."

Jacie blushed. "I *knew* it!"

Tyler stared at her. "How many times do we have to go through this? You're a great artist."

Jacie looked at him, determined to know in spite of any discomfort. She bored her eyes into his, daring him to tell the truth.

"Look," Tyler said, leaning toward her and putting his hand on her ankle. "I know you think we're all just being nice. But why would we do that? What about your grand prize? Why would we let our closest friend traipse off to an artist conference if we thought she'd make a fool of herself? That's not being a friend."

Jacie felt her face warm, and she looked down at her soda again, drawing her fingernail around and around the groove. How many times had they not told Tyler about his inability to sing on key?

Tyler lifted her chin. "I know."

"Know what?" Jacie asked, feeling like he'd again read her soul. *How does he do that?*

"You don't think I know how awful I sound when I sing?"

Jacie felt quite like a fish, opening and closing her mouth. Probably looking really stupid.

Tyler threw his head back and started to laugh. "I've known for a while—back when I recorded myself trying to start that band." He shook his head. "Horrible stuff." He looked her in the eyes again. "Why didn't you ever tell me?"

Jacie shrugged. Her voice came out very small. "I didn't know how to tell you, because your music is good—really good. It's just your singing that's, well, um—"

"Look, Jacie. Listen to things you guys have said about my music, and listen to what everyone has said about your art. Do you hear a difference?"

Jacie sucked some soda, and thought. What *had* the others said and done? Had anyone ever entered Tyler in a voice contest? *No. But Hannah entered my art.* Had anyone ever said anything positive to Tyler when he talked about becoming a famous rock star? *No.* They'd all looked at each other and let the comments pass. They didn't remark on his dreams at all. Not a word. Yet her friends continually encouraged her to draw, to paint.

"I do hear a difference," she said, her voice catching in her chest. It felt like she spoke a lie.

Tyler reached over and tugged on her arm until she relaxed and let him pull her toward him. He stopped when they were knee to knee. He took the soda can from her hand, putting it and his Dr Pepper onto the battered coffee table. He took both her hands in his. "You are incredible."

His breath came at her, dark and warm with bubbles. A hint of Dr Pepper.

He massaged her hands a little, her heart picking up the beat.

"I'm not that good," she whispered.

"You are *so* good. You are an amazing girl, Jacie."

"It's just what I like to do."

Tyler swallowed so hard, Jacie could see.

"Jacie. You don't understand. It's *all* of you that's amazing. Your heart. How you see life. How you aren't afraid to question God. How you cling to God anyway. I feel so stupid for seeing you only as a sister for the past . . . well, for lots of years."

Jacie thought she should pull her hands away. But that would feel like taking herself back and leaving Tyler somewhere out there, floating. She wanted to be connected with him. It was so scary, but something she wanted. Something she realized she'd wanted for a long time. But she always thought she wasn't good enough. Or that it was wrong, very wrong, to want it.

"Tyler," Tyra whined, bouncing into the room. "I told you I want to borrow your Animalectronica CD. I *have* to know—" She stopped, staring at them. "Did you guys kiss or something?"

Could Tyra read her desires? Had she really wanted to kiss him? Were those the thoughts clashing with his words, making it hard for her to think? Why would she want to kiss Tyler? Jacie's attempt to suppress a laugh came out in a hiccup.

She looked at Tyler and noticed his cheeks were flaming pink. "No," he said a bit harshly. "Jacie and I have never kissed."

Tyra rolled her eyes, popping out one hip and placing an indignant hand on it. "Well, you should. You guys are sooo made for—"

"The CD is on my bed."

"No, it's not. I looked."

"You're not supposed to be in my room."

"Well, I was. And it's not on your bed."

"Under the black notebook."

"Oh, you mean the one with Jacie's name all over it?"

Jacie tilted her head, staring at him, smiling, her heart revving up for something.

He looked at Jacie. "No such notebook exists, all right?"

Tyra giggled. "No, but it should—"

Tyler threw a pillow at her and she dodged it and skipped out of the room.

Jacie didn't know what to say. Much of her wanted to tell Tyler what was going on inside. She wanted to tell him that things were getting mixed up and she didn't know what she wanted or didn't want. She wanted to lean over and kiss him—finally. But why? This was Tyler Jennings. Why would she want to do that?

Ever since Dinah's death, she felt a bit like she did after experiencing an earthquake in California. Her footing unstable, her mind rattled and confused. It was like a snow globe with pieces of everything floating around.

"You came here to tell me some news. It's not bad news, is it? We've had enough of that this year."

"I—" At that moment Jacie wondered if it *was* bad news. She'd been thinking how great it would be. But now, in the light of real life, was it good news or bad news?

Tyler took a swig of his Dr Pepper, waiting patiently.

"Mrs. R asked me to teach an art class at the Community Center!"

"No way."

"Way. And I start next Thursday." Jacie waited for more reaction.

"Jacie! That's fabulous! Think of how that will look on a

résumé." Tyler slammed his Dr Pepper on the coffee table with a thud that caused droplets to fly out of the can and rain onto the table. He leaned forward and threw his arms around her. For a moment Jacie felt lost. Polo Sport. Laundry soap. Shampoo. *Tyler.* She jerked her mind back to the moment and gave him a couple of taps on the back. She hoped that would suffice for a return hug.

At least in snow globes everything stays inside.

• • •

Jacie pulled her car into her carport spot, watching carefully for toy mines that might be placed about. Sure enough, there was a plastic Barney and a naked Barbie doll placed in strategic spots for unsuspecting drivers. She carefully maneuvered by them as she had the orange cones during driver training. She opened her door, gathered her stuff, and got out, kicking the door shut with her foot.

As she came around the edge of the carport, Nora stood not 15 feet away, sticking her tongue out at Jacie. Then she spun around and ran into the house screaming. "Maaa-maaa," she wailed. Right before she slammed the door, she poked her head through and stuck her tongue out a second time.

Jacie marveled at how well this kid could make such an ugly face between wails that to the untrained ear would seem endless.

She took a deep breath and mounted the stairs to the townhouse. She unlocked the door. Her mom stood there, holding out the phone. "It's for you," she said, shaking the cordless at her. "Solana."

"What did you do now?" Solana demanded.

"I don't know what you're talking about." Jacie shrugged her shoulders at her mom's questioning eyes and moved to her bedroom. She closed the door gently with her foot and dropped onto the floor by her bed.

"It's all over town," Solana said.

Jacie felt her brain scramble. "That I ran over Mickey Mouse?" Jacie asked, thinking about Nora's plump, pink tongue and ear-piercing wails and shrieks.

"EWWW!" Solana said. "Did you really? That's disgusting."

"A *toy*, Sol. A bratty kid who—"

"You're calling a kid bratty? Now that's news."

Jacie sighed, her brain too muddled by the events of the past two hours to make sense of much of anything. "What's all over town, Sol?"

"That Mrs. R wanted to see you. We all know that's trouble."

"Not always."

"So?"

"Becca didn't tell you?"

"Becca doesn't know why Mrs. R wanted to see you. You know Mrs. R won't say a word to anyone else about her business."

"How do you know so much about Mrs. R? You hardly ever show up at the Community Center."

Solana sighed. Jacie knew that particular sigh quite well. It meant that Solana couldn't believe the stupidity of the person she was sighing at—which at this moment was Jacie. "I'm not deaf, you know. I *am* Becca's friend. I *do* hear you guys talking about Mrs. R endlessly."

Jacie shook her head, glad Solana couldn't see her own frustration. "Yeah, yeah."

"So? What'd she want to rake you over the coals for?"

"Well, Sol. Guess you don't know Mrs. R that well. She called me in to ask me to teach an art class."

"She *did*? Well it's about time, Jace. You're perfect for it. Let me know if you need any help—"

"Wow, Sol, that's really—"

"—and I'll recruit Hannah."

Jacie started laughing.

"It might help her, too."

"Why, Solana. You sound downright concerned."

Instead of acting snotty, Solana said in a soft voice few people had ever heard, "I am. She's really scaring me. Not talking much. She's going to get a permanent wrinkle between her perfect eyebrows if she doesn't stop concentrating so hard. Those drippy tears she's always trying to hide are beginning to unnerve me. What are we going to do? I almost wish we had Holy Hannah back. I miss her pat answers. At least they were Hannah."

"Do you want the canned adult answer or my answer?"

"Yours. Of course."

"I don't know what to do, either, Solana. I can't tell her to trust God because I don't trust Him."

"You don't?"

Jacie sighed. "How can I trust a God who would throw pregnant, wonderful Aunt Dinah into a ravine? She was only trying to serve Him, for goodness' sake!"

Solana was quiet for some time. Jacie didn't have anything more to say anyway. She chewed on her bottom lip, pulling the dry skin off.

Solana's voice became husky. "I don't know what to do when all my friends who've believed in God forever suddenly don't believe in Him anymore. It kinda freaks me out."

"Our worlds are turning upside down, aren't they?"

"Yeah. In different ways."

"What are we going to do?"

Jacie wondered if, in the silence, Solana was shrugging her shoulders. "You know, Jace. I'd never admit I said this . . . but . . . if God is who you say He is, maybe He'll sort it out for you sooner or later."

Jacie started to cry little drippy tears herself. She hated losing God. But right now she hated the God who killed Aunt

Dinah. It was like He backed over her and didn't think twice about it. Did He discard Dinah into the ravine like a plastic doll—a toy He was no longer interested in playing with? She tried to stuff the ugly thoughts into a tin box inside her soul. But every time she did, they popped out and frightened her like a tinkly jack-in-the-box.

How in the world would this ever make sense?

chapter 5

Some days Jacie felt perfectly normal. Sloshing through alternately new and melting snow at school, trying not to slip on the ice. Talking with friends, eating, throwing bits of food at each other, laughing at stupid jokes, talking about classes and people and teachers, and planning the future. But it was when they started talking about the future that Jacie started to feel the anxiety creep in through her middle and climb up to slither around her brain and begin to squeeze. She felt like everything should go black. Isn't that what happened in stories? In the movies you could see a faint coming on the face of the actress: the blank stare, holding her breath, gone.

But nothing went black. It did, however, seem to go in slow motion. Or like Jacie had suddenly zoomed backwards and could see everything at a distance. Little voices chattered in her mind—finches trying to get at what little grains of food were sprinkled there.

Future? What future?

Does this future involve God? As if He *can be trusted.*

Train cars falling, falling, smashing in a ravine.

God has a wonderful plan for your life.

God is good—all the time.

Eat, drink, and be merry, for tomorrow you die.

Jacie shook her head, her springy curls gently boinging against her cheeks.

"—wants to help Otis?" Becca's voice brought Jacie back to what she thought might be the current reality. Becca had a pen poised over a small spiral notebook with *Nate* etched in every spare corner of the covers.

"When?" Tyler asked, shoveling a Chipotle burrito into his mouth.

"Those are not real burritos," Solana complained. "They just make you think they are."

"I dumph caph—" Tyler muffled, his mouth overfull with burrito.

"Gross!" Solana said.

Tyler opened his mouth wide, letting some gooey morsels dribble out.

"You are so disgusting. I was going to comment on how mature you've been lately."

"Is everyone ignoring me?" Becca asked.

"Pretty much," Solana said.

Hannah stared across the quad, her face a mask. Sometimes it seemed Hannah didn't exist any more.

Jacie kind of missed the old Hannah. She missed that she could ask her a question and pretty much get an answer she expected. Sol was right. Now you never knew what would come out of her mouth—if anything.

"I'll help," Hannah said, her voice barely a whisper. She turned, her body mechanical.

"O-kay," Becca said, making wide-eyes at everyone else. "I'll put an enthusiastic YES! from Hannah."

"You don't even know when," Tyler said, wiping his mouth.

"I don't care when," Hannah said. "It doesn't matter."

Jacie could hear the rest that remained unsaid. *Nothing matters anymore.*

She wished she could argue with Hannah. She wished she could do what Hannah used to do for them—encourage them to look up. But she felt just like Hannah.

Nothing matters anymore.

• • •

On Thursday afternoon, Jacie didn't know whether her tremors were about being afraid of teaching, excited about teaching, or not having enough to eat. All she knew was that every part of her shook. She could swear her liver was even quivering—if she knew where her liver was.

Mrs. R had called. She didn't have enough stuff, so Jacie looped eight plastic grocery bags of art supplies over her arms. Feeling like a squishy bag lady, she used every ounce of concentration to cautiously step down the stairs of the townhouse.

"I hate you."

Jacie stopped. She closed her eyes and took a deep breath. She opened them to the inevitable fat, pink tongue. "Hi, Nora."

"I said, 'I *hate* you.'"

Jacie knew what she wanted to say. That she hated Nora, too. She wanted to be three feet high at this moment, wearing some sort of orangish pants outfit like Nora's, and sass her back just as much as the little girl sassed her. She could see them sassing louder and louder back and forth until someone's mother came out and told them to quit. They'd both stick their tongues out at each other and turn and flounce away.

Oh, the pleasures of flouncing. Jacie couldn't do that

anymore. She was nearly 18 and supposed to be done with flouncing.

"Didn't you hear me?" Nora shrieked.

"I heard you, Nora," Jacie said, her voice sounding an awful lot like her mother's did when she was weary of Jacie's childish outbursts.

"Whatcha gonna do about it?"

Jacie started to step carefully down the stairs again. "Nothing."

Nora put her hands on her hips, her face screwed into total indignation. "But I hate you," she said, her voice demanding.

"I know, Nora." Jacie shifted the weight of the bags on her right arm. It felt like one would slice through the skin if she didn't off-load it soon. "Here," she said, taking the offending bag and handing it to Nora. "You can carry it for me."

Nora looked at the bag in her hand. "What is it?"

"Art supplies."

Nora's face brightened. "Really?" She pulled the handles apart and peeked inside. Bottles of colored glitter. Confetti in the shapes of dogs, horses, children, words. Colored paper. Shiny paper. And a couple bottles of primary-colored tempera paint. "Wow," she breathed. "What's it for?"

"An art class," Jacie said. "Do you want to come?"

Jacie immediately wanted to stuff the words back into her mouth, and Nora remembered she was talking to the Mickey-killer. Nora dropped the bag. "I'm not gonna help you! And you can't make me! I'm gonna tell my mom!"

Jacie watched in detached awe as Nora clenched her fists, scrunched up her face, held her breath just long enough to turn her face beet red, then let it all out in an ear-piercing wail. "M-o-o-m-m-m-y!" She ran full bore to her house.

Jacie didn't have time to find out what was going to happen this time. She was already late for her planned setup time for class. She scooped up the dropped bag. It split, sending glitter and confetti bottles in different directions. The paper, thankfully, remained inside. Wailing in the background matched the wailing in her head. Could she run to Mommy and complain? She wished she could. But there was no one to complain to. Even God ignored her.

She gathered the bottles and containers, stuffed them into other bags, and scuttled toward her car. The door groaned; she dropped the bags behind the driver's seat, slid inside and closed the door. Key turned. Ignition started. Engine running. Reverse. No crunching sounds. Continue on.

The little brat is taking over my life. I can't do anything right. Even when I'm nice she thinks I'm an ogre. This kid complained about everything. She was determined to see Jacie as the bad guy no matter what she did.

I refuse to let her ruin my day.

I refuse to think about her.

But she *did* think about her. She paid virtually no attention to her driving. Her brain and car, both on automatic pilot, got her to the Community Center without an accident or ticket, both of which she may have deserved.

She glanced at her watch. Only 15 minutes until her class started. There was so much to do!

Angela signed her in and directed her to the classroom. All the classrooms at the temporary Community Center were fairly dull. They had to accommodate people of all ages, so most of the stuff kids might find stimulating had to be replaced by posters and pictures and quotes that no one would find particularly stimulating.

Her own classroom had posters of quiet seascapes at sunset, non-threatening clouds, and other sedate nature scenes with inspirational captions underneath. There was a drawing of some old guy with a quote underneath him as well, each letter cut from a different color of construction paper, and pinned to the wall. Jacie didn't have time to decipher it all.

She quickly unrolled butcher paper along the long tables, fastening them underneath with cheap tape that would hold probably just until the students arrived.

She set out glue, safety-tipped scissors, paper, and a million kinds of doodads that one could paste onto paper: string, macaroni, bottle caps, Styrofoam peanuts, beads, confetti, glitter, old jewelry, buttons, and a bunch of odds and ends she'd been throwing into a box for years.

When she was done, she stood back and took a deep breath. *Teaching*. What a concept! She, Jacie Noland, teaching her favorite subject.

At precisely 4:00 P.M., the classroom door opened. Jacie stiffened into what she hoped looked like a real teacher's posture. Mrs. R walked in. Her all-encompassing gaze assessed the room. She gave one nod. "Looks good. Be done by 5:00, please. Clean up—15 minutes. These folks need to get to the common room for the program and dinner." She spun on her heels and clicked out.

Jacie sat behind the desk, folding her hands and placing them on the worn wood. She smiled at the empty room. She stood, took a piece of chalk, and wrote her name: Miss Noland. She drew cows in beds of flowers, some heads bent, faces disappearing into the blooms. She drew and smudged, stood back to analyze, then looked closely again.

"I ain't never gonna draw like that, Teacher," a small voice said.

Jacie spun around to see five kids and three adults staring at her and the blackboard. "Oh, I'm sorry. I didn't see—"

The door opened, and fumbling and bumping ensued as a bulky wheelchair appeared. Sitting in it was a little girl who would have been darling if she hadn't been drooling all over herself. Her slack mouth hung open, her chin touching a large quilted bib that matched her bright pink corduroy overalls. A stretchy cord of drool went from the corner of her mouth to the bib. Her right arm seemed tied by an invisible rope to her chest. Her fingers curled like a claw. Her left arm and hand waved about as if a puppeteer controlled them.

The children backed away from her, fear of catching whatever disease contorted her body written on their faces. The adults turned away, walking about the room as if terribly interested in the posters and words of wisdom.

"This here's Marlene," the woman pushing the chair said. "They told me I could leave her here so she could get some art. Don't worry none about her wetting herself or nothing. She's got diapers. She's my daughter Sarah's girl. Sarah'll come get her after work." The grandmother looked at Marlene. "You be good, okay?"

Guttural sounds came out of the girl. The grandmother started to laugh. "Ain't she a hoot? That girl keeps me laughing."

A thousand questions flooded Jacie's mind: *Did she really just say something? Can she talk? Does she understand me? Is her mind okay and just her body not working? How can she do art? What am I supposed to do with her?* "Okay," was all that she managed to squeak out.

God, she managed to shoot out a prayer. *Do something. Help me.*

chapter 6

Jacie managed to gather everyone around the long table and find out their names. She didn't know what to do with Marlene, so she pushed her chair up to the table. The table was far too low for Marlene's wheelchair, but she left her there anyway. Marlene seemed to track with some of the names, and then seemed to disappear into some place inside herself. Jacie sat next to her, but "around the corner" from her end of the table so she could watch. Marlene's head wagged and drooped. Sometimes it seemed Marlene had control over it, but at other times it seemed her head was simply too heavy for her neck to hold upright.

When Gina and Ricky punched each other good-naturedly, Marlene's mouth opened to a huge grin, and she made a sucking guffaw. Obviously it was a laugh—which stopped Gina and Ricky cold.

"What was *that*?" Ricky asked.

“She laughed, you dumbhead,” Gina told him.

“I’m not a dumbhead. You are.”

Marlene guffawed again.

Brenda, a tall, leggy woman with stringy blonde hair falling to her thin waist, leaned forward and stared at Marlene.

Marlene uttered noises. A sentence? Some noises sounded like they might be words.

Brenda drew back, as if she’d encountered a gruesome character in a horror movie. She turned her chair so that she couldn’t see Marlene. “What are you going to teach us?” she asked Jacie.

“I thought, um, maybe this time, this week . . . we’d like to put some things on paper.” The students stared at her. She swallowed. Sweated. Shifted from one foot to the other.

“See? I have all these things.” She waved her arm to indicate all the doodads she’d collected. “You can glue them onto paper and see how artistic you can be with stuff that . . . um . . . you wouldn’t think of as being artistic.” Inside she groaned at how lame she sounded. “While you create, I want to find out what you want to learn. Next week we’ll probably start drawing.”

“I can’t draw,” Brenda said.

“Me neither,” Joe said.

“That’s why I’m here,” Jacie tried to say patiently.

Joe sat straight in the chair, an air of distinguished gentleman about him. He didn’t have the stooped shoulders of one beaten down by a long period of homelessness. “I trust you can teach anyone.”

Jacie tried not to look at his well-toned biceps. She felt stupid that this man could flatter her with a look, a flexed bicep, and a kind word.

While her students began to pass around the bottles of glue, making interesting designs with the elements in front of them, Jacie took note that she’d like to bring in some GDs. The quiet felt awkward. Even Ricky looked up a few times, as if he'd like to say something but couldn't break the silence. Marlene made snuffling noises and seemed to be shouting occasional words.

Jacie looked at her and wondered if she wanted to make something. She sat next to her and asked, but Marlene's head lolled around on top of her neck.

Jacie put a piece of orange construction paper on Marlene's tray. She took a bottle of glue and put it into Marlene's right hand.

Big mistake.

The spastic muscles squeezed a stream of glue onto her left hand, then the bottle flew across the tray, landing on the table.

"Good one!" Ricky applauded.

Marlene guffawed.

Brenda turned to look, then spun away again, cringing against Marlene's uncomfortable presence.

Marlene's glue-covered hand waved about of its own accord, swiping glue on her hair, clothes, and ear. Jacie finally came to her senses and grabbed Marlene's wrist. Then she didn't know what to do with it once she'd captured it.

Marlene's mouth hung open wide. Delight shone like sunshine on her face. Her head wagged from side to side.

"You're lookin' good, Marlene," Ricky said.

A noise raked across Marlene's throat sounding like cloth rubbed across an old-fashioned washboard.

"Gina, could you please get me some wet paper towels?"

She took off like a flash, returning moments later with a wad of towels.

"Thanks." Jacie dabbed at Marlene, who moaned something.

The kids had grown bored with Marlene's hand-painting efforts and were grabbing items from across the table or down the way, gluing them onto colored sheets of paper. The adults seemed uninterested in their artistic tasks, and Jacie felt locked between cleaning up Marlene and being a teacher to the others.

"Ricky," she said, "go to the desk and bring over the collages I've made."

Ricky obliged, returning to the long tables with a short stack of construction paper art pieces in his hand. "Look!" he said, holding up the top one. "Lookit whatchu can do."

Everyone stopped and stared at the picture of a girl's face that Jacie had done with different items she'd brought. Tiny black buttons represented tightly curled hair. Elbow macaroni outlined her face, which had bottle caps for eyes. Jacie was proud of it. Anyone could tell it was a little girl.

Brenda dropped the sequins she'd been painstakingly working with. "I can't do that. All I can do is junk."

Joe stared at the picture, then looked down at his own gluey mess. The others around the table looked at their pictures with despair, and then at those around them.

"Wait!" Jacie said, tossing the paper towels into the trash. "Look at these." She held up other things she'd done, ones that didn't look so much like a piece of art. They were just fun pieces playing with color and form.

Brenda shook her head. "I can't even do one of those."

Jacie looked at the paper she held up. The geometric swirls blended and moved through the color spectrum. She had never thought that what she did for fun would cause others to feel inadequate.

"It doesn't matter," Jacie said. "Just glue things the way you want them. Express your heart through your work. What is it that you feel?"

"Stupid," Brenda said under her breath.

A few others nodded their heads.

Jacie wanted to nod along with them. She felt stupid too. I mean, how hard was it to teach art? She knew all about art, didn't she? She could do this.

Now, more than ever, she wished she had brought music. At least then she could tell them to create what they felt from the music.

She sighed and dropped herself into a chair. She began to grab sequins and pasta and string and bottle caps. She lost herself in putting things together. Creating her frustration on paper. The result looked awful. But who cared? Frustration *is* awful.

"Look what I did!" Gina said. She held up her paper and showed it around. A rainfall of glitter drifted onto the table. In rainbow and glitter letters, the words said, "God loves you and me."

The adults looked and nodded; the kids didn't seem to care. But Marlene suddenly started making all kinds of weird moaning noises. Everyone stopped and stared at her. Brenda put her hands over her ears and crouched low to the table.

Marlene's arms waved all around with great force. She would have decked the nearest person had there been anyone next to her.

"Do you think she's trying to talk?" Joe asked.

Jacie stared at her, trying hard to make sense of the moans. And then, she could hear it. "Gaw uuvvs yo ang may."

Jacie looked from Marlene to the paper. Marlene's tear-filled eyes fixed on the green construction paper. "She's reading," Jacie whispered.

"Wow," Ricky said. "She's not such a dummy after all."

Gina smacked him with the back of her hand. "Shut up. You're the dummy."

The spell was broken. Marlene's eyes went dark and her head drooped on the stem of her neck like a wilting flower. Her arms pinned themselves to her body.

Brenda looked up tentatively, slowly taking her hands from her ears. She stared at her own art design and frowned.

Jacie looked at the clock, hoping time was up. But only a little more than half an hour had passed. She knew she'd have to have more instruction next time. Something. Or she would die of boredom and frustration. She took a deep breath and prayed a silent prayer. *God, help.*

She walked around the table and looked over the shoulders of her students. "That looks good. I like the colors you're choosing."

"What a cute little dog. He looks like he'd be fun to play with."

"Look at that house! I could live there."

Cheesy, cheesier, cheesiest, she complained to herself. Couldn't she think of something better to say?

She looked at her watch, hoping it would rescue her from this torture.

Ten more minutes had passed.

Jacie didn't know what to do with Marlene. She'd better ask more questions next time. She sat at the opposite end of the table and watched her. The more Jacie looked at Marlene, the more she thought about Dinah. Sheesh. Did all roads lead to Dinah? It sure seemed like it. She was sick of obsessing over Dinah. Sick of thinking about it all the time. Sick of everything reminding her of Dinah. But here it was again. Marlene. Alive, but basically dead. She couldn't do a single thing for herself. Could barely communicate. Couldn't draw. Couldn't pick up anything. Couldn't even hold her head up. What kind of life was that?

What was God thinking?

"Teacher," Brenda said, "I don't know if I'm going to come back. I didn't really learn anything."

"I promise," Jacie said, fear coming out in tiny pricks on the palms of her hands and in her stomach, "next week I'll teach you the basics of how to draw. It will be fun."

"What if I can't do that either?"

"At least you'll try, right?" She hoped she didn't sound like she was begging.

Brenda shrugged. When she picked up her soggy paper and left, the others followed her. Except for Marlene. And Gina.

"Can I help you clean up?" Gina asked.

Jacie smiled. "I'd love it, thanks."

"You're Becca's friend, aren't you?"

"Yeah."

"I like her. She's fun."

"Yeah, she is."

Gina walked around, scooping macaroni into the Tupperware container. "Marlene has dinner with us sometimes."

"She does? She's homeless?"

"No. They just don't have very much money."

Jacie closed all the glue containers and wiped the tops with a corner of the paper she'd covered the tables with. She needed to bring a damp cloth in a Ziploc next week. But then next week she wasn't bringing glue. She would bring pencils, charcoal, oil pastels—something like that.

"She eats kind of sloppy," Gina said.

"She eats by herself?"

"No. That lady feeds her. But she still gets it all over the place. I guess cuz she can't hold her head still."

"Does she talk much?"

Gina shrugged. She covered the macaroni and started on the foil confetti. "This is the first time I've heard her. But no one talks to her."

Jacie took out the cardboard box and began to stow the supplies in it. It felt weird talking about someone when she was sitting right there. But Marlene seemed to be gone somewhere no one else could visit.

"Do you think God really loves Marlene?"

Jacie felt as if someone had taken her breath away. What should she tell this child? She didn't want to destroy her faith. And she honestly didn't know the right answer. "Why do you ask?"

Gina went right up to Marlene's chair and looked at her. It wasn't an unkind stare, but it was as if she were trying to communicate with her nonverbally. Or as if she were trying to see inside Marlene and understand her. "Well," Gina said, touching Marlene's finger, then another, then holding her hand. "If God loves us and wants the best for us, why does He put someone in a body like Marlene's? It doesn't seem very fair, does it?"

"No," Jacie said. "It doesn't."

"So? Why did God make her like this?"

Jacie felt as if she were rummaging around in old, musty boxes in an attic somewhere, looking for truth amongst the other riffraff of life. "I don't know," she said. "But maybe we don't really understand what God's love is like. If we did, we wouldn't think twice about Marlene . . . or anyone else like her."

Gina seemed to accept this answer. And the shocking thing was, Jacie believed it too. She didn't understand it. But she felt, in the center of her being, that it was true.

chapter 7

Jacie's mom stood in the kitchen doorway, the light behind her shining around her head like some old *Touched by an Angel* episode. She wiped her hands on her apron—quite unlike an angel. "How was your first day?"

Jacie shrugged. "Not so good."

"I'm sorry."

"It's okay. I'll do better next week." She didn't really want to talk about it yet. She needed to process what went wrong a little more. Besides, her mom obviously had something else on her mind. She stood there grinning and squirming like an eager little kid.

"Well, I have some news," her mom said.

Jacie had a devious thought to torment her a little. "Okay, but I have to pee so bad I'm about ready to explode. I'll be back in a minute."

"Well, hurry!" her mom said, bouncing on her feet.

Jacie plodded up the stairs, making her footsteps clunk up each one. She was being cruel and she knew it. But, ahhh, what delicious cruelty! She loved how she and her mom could tease each other. She loved that her mom would tease right back. She got offended only when Jacie teased about the truth, or about someone who needed to be shown more kindness.

Jacie dropped her purse and keys onto the bed, then went to the top of the stairs and called down. "Mom, I think it might be a bit of an extended visit."'

"JACIE NOLAND! Get back down here pronto or my death will be on your head," her mom yelled from the kitchen.

"Nah. You're an adult. You won't die."

The apron flew through the kitchen doorway as if it could round the corner, travel up the stairs, and hit her.

Jacie went into the bathroom and took her time. She picked up a magazine. *Reader's Digest.* She flipped open to "Life in These United States," laughing out loud at many of the stories. When she finished, she clunked back down the stairs.

"Well?" she asked her mom. She dropped into a chair at the kitchen table and picked up a flyer.

Her mother spun around, water droplets from the bubbled dishwater flying through the air. "Yes!" she said, stabbing a finger at the flyer. "What do you think?"

"What do I think about what?"

"That!" her mother shouted, again pointing at the flyer.

Jacie looked down at the home-drawn, photocopied flyer. *Front Range Animal Rescue*. She shrugged. "I guess it's nice that they use animals to rescue people." She cocked her head. "You need rescuing?"

"Ha-ha," her mother intoned. "Very funny." Then she got her excited, little-girl voice again. "It's an organization that has foster care for unwanted animals until they can find a permanent home for them."

She didn't want to sound rude, but she didn't get it. "Okay."

Jacie's mom dragged a chair out from the table and sat in it. "I'm going to get a dog." She beamed.

Jacie felt her jaw drop open. There was no way her mother was getting a dog. It was a joke.

"I went to the pet store today," her mother continued. "Front Range takes dogs and cats to local pet stores for a couple hours and they let you choose. I didn't find one I like yet, but I know I will."

Jacie still stared at her mother.

Her mother slipped the flyer from Jacie's hand. "Won't that be fun?"

Jacie still didn't know what to say. She pictured a big, hairy dog in their small townhouse. She liked dogs. Well. Maybe. She'd never had one. She gave up begging for one years ago.

"I'm thinking a Lab mix," her mother said. "Some kind of dog that is really loyal and friendly and playful."

"Mom," Jacie said softly, trying to measure her words so they wouldn't sound mean. "Why are you getting a dog?"

Her mother's cheeks pinked. She shrugged her shoulders, stood up from the chair, and went back to her dishes. "I thought it might be nice for us to have a dog."

"Why?" Jacie repeated.

Her mom stopped. She took a deep breath, then continued. "You're leaving in less than a year, Jacie. It's always been just you and I. What will I do when you're gone? I'm going to be so lonely." She picked up a pot and began to scrub furiously.

Jacie still didn't know what to say. Her mom *lonely*? "But you have so many friends. How could you be lonely?"

Looking over her shoulder, Jacie's mom continued to scrub. "They don't live here. I want someone else breathing in this house. I want someone to say good night to. I want someone to talk to."

Jacie rolled her eyes. "You aren't going to become one of those old women who are creepy about their dogs, are you? Talk baby talk. Put sweaters on them. Dress them up for Halloween."

"I don't intend to become 'creepy.' But I do intend to train the dog to be well behaved and will consider it my buddy for hiking as well as other things."

Jacie shook her head. "Mom. You don't hike."

"I'm going to begin. I found some hiking boots my size at Goodwill today. I bought some socks at Target. There's a hiking group I might join. But with a dog, I can hike with or without a group."

The smell of something warm seeped from the oven and filled the kitchen. Jacie got up and reached for two ratty terrycloth potholders. She opened the oven and looked at the casserole inside. "Is it ready?"

"Bubbling? Brown?"

"Both."

"It's ready."

Jacie lifted it from the oven and put it on the stovetop. "It smells really good."

"I got lazy and made chicken enchiladas all mushed together."

Jacie nodded. She opened a cabinet and took out two plates. She got silverware from a drawer and set it all on the kitchen table with multicolored placemats and a basket with napkins in the center.

She hadn't thought of her mother being alone before. Weren't moms immune to loneliness? Didn't their work and kids make up for it?

Someone pounded on the front door. Jacie set down the water glass by the knife and went to answer it.

"Greetings!" Solana said. "I come bearing friends."

Jacie looked around her and saw Hannah, Becca, and Tyler pounding up the stairs behind her.

"Who's the brat?" Solana asked, jerking her thumb behind her.

Jacie looked down the stairs and saw Nora doing a sort of wildly flapping bizarre chicken dance, her tongue lolling about. Jacie waved. "Hi, Nora! Got any toys you want me to run over today?"

Nora's tongue disappeared. She jerked her head straight back, looking like a chicken who'd stopped mid-strut. Her eyes widened.

"Come on in," Jacie said to her friends, moving to one side. "Don't worry about her. She's a weird kid."

"Smells fab," Tyler said, his nose poking the air and sniffing. Jacie pictured him with fur, dangly ears, and a jingling collar. She could see it as clearly as if she'd just drawn it. She'd never be able to really pay attention to anything until she drew the picture—weird as it was.

"Come on in," Jacie's mom said, standing in the kitchen door. "Jacie, set the table in the dining room."

"We didn't mean to interrupt dinner," Tyler said.

"Yes you did," Solana said. "You said, 'Let's go to Jacie's house. I bet Ms. N is about to put out one of her yummy casseroles.' "

"I did not," Tyler protested.

Hannah ignored them. "Can I help, Ms. N? We really didn't expect you to have dinner."

"We wanted to steal Jacie away to Señor Taco," Becca said, "to find out how the art class went."

"She's mine tonight," Ms. Noland said. "But I'd be happy to have all of you here."

Dinner commenced with prayer and fast conversation, beginning with Jacie telling them all about the disastrous class. Jacie loved when her friends came over. Her mother came alive, bantering, challenging, teasing. She never tried to be one of them, but she always interacted as though all of them were her children.

As Jacie watched, participated, and listened, she didn't like the realization that was sneaking up on her. Before it took full root inside, she smashed it. "Mom's getting a dog," she blurted.

"Really?" Hannah asked. "What kind?"

The conversation spun around dogs and the pros and cons of which breeds, their shedding hair, needing walks, and making messes. Mostly, everyone thought it was a great idea.

Everyone but me, Jacie thought, quietly kicking herself. Why was it that she felt something surging inside. What was that?

JEALOUSY?

The idea shocked her. But the truth of it shocked her even more. How could she be jealous of a stupid dog? Especially a dog they didn't even have yet. She wondered how much one of those roller things that pick up dog hairs would cost.

The doorbell rang. Jacie got up to answer it, and her friends didn't stop the conversation for a second. Nora stood there, a tall red-and-white-striped *Cat in the Hat* hat upon her head. A plastic Cinderella mask covered her face, the golden yellow hair failing to hide Nora's brunette hair behind it. She clutched a small brown sack with handles in both hands. "Trick or treat," Nora said.

"Excuse me?" Jacie said.

"Trick or treat," Nora said, her voice muffled behind the mask.

"It's not Halloween."

"Trick or TREAT," Nora said, her voice insistent.

Jacie stood there, not knowing what to do.

Nora shifted her weight and tapped her foot impatiently.

"Just a minute," Jacie said, turning away.

"Who is it?" Jacie's mom asked.

"The brat from downstairs," Jacie said through gritted teeth. "She's dressed up and saying, 'Trick or treat.' "

"How cute," Becca said. "Are you going to give her something?"

"Of course she is," Mrs. Noland said, already leaving her chair for the kitchen.

"But, Mom, she'll be back every night for more."

"I don't care."

"But she's such a pest."

Mrs. Noland disappeared into the kitchen and returned with two Oreos. "Tell her it's all we have. That's the truth."

Jacie took the Oreos and stared at them.

"Don't be this way, Jacie. She's just a little girl pretending. Besides, you went trick-or-treating a lot when you were about her age."

"I did?"

"Sure. It was like the idea got stuck in your head and you thought this was something kids could do whenever they wanted candy."

"How embarrassing."

Tyler grabbed her free hand and swung it. "You can trick-or-treat at my house any time you want." He lifted his eyebrows as if he were a leering old man.

"Shut up."

Jacie returned to the front door. "Here," she said, dropping the cookies into the bag. Even through the mask's eye holes, Jacie could see Nora's eyes widen. Nora followed the path of the cookies from Jacie's hand into the bag as if completely disbelieving her good fortune. She turned and walked down the stairs—both feet touching each stair. The moment she reached the bottom, she broke into a dead run screaming at the top of her lungs, "MOMMY! MOMMY! MOMMY!" Only this time it wasn't a phony wail.

Jacie closed the door, laughing inside.

Everyone joined in to clean the tiny kitchen, which made it look like a bumper car amusement. Tyler began to putter around like a car, running into everyone on purpose, backing up and starting again.

"Tyler!" Solana shrieked. "We are not in middle school."

Tyler turned red and stopped. "Just playing."

"Playing is a good thing," Hannah said.

Tyler smiled gratefully, his embarrassment still hanging around his body language. "I'm sorry, Sol. I really am trying to grow up."

Solana gave him a hug. "I guess we're all a little overly sensitive lately," she said.

Becca hung up the tea towel. "I'm done. I've got homework to do. Ty, you taking us home?"

"Of course," he said.

"Jacie, would you mind taking me home?" Hannah asked. "I've got some photos I'd like your opinion on. I want to do something really artistic for the next newspaper issue. I thought we could do something creative together."

Jacie looked at her mom.

"Go!" her mom said. "Just be home by 10."

● ● ●

After Jacie had waded through the Connor family greetings, she and Hannah went upstairs to Hannah's attic room. Hannah flopped onto her bed and Jacie took the wicker rocker. "What's the theme?"

"I've got three coming up. First will be a sort of historical collage of the senior class. You know, mostly middle school through senior year. I need it to be symbolic more than anything; otherwise, there's way too much material."

"Gotcha."

"Then we'll be doing one on prom and pre-graduation."

"Okay. So how 'bout some sort of theme that ties them all together? Some sort of banner or border that goes along with it? I could design one pretty quickly."

"Okay," Hannah said, reaching underneath her bed for a cardboard box. She stuck her hand in and removed an envelope. Inside were stacks of black-and-white photos. She held them a moment, then tapped them on her hand.

"Jacie?" Hannah asked, her voice quiet and contemplative. She dropped her hands to her lap and looked at Jacie, fixing her with her gaze. "If you knew your death would cause many people to come to know Christ, would you allow God to do it?"

Jacie took a deep breath. *So here is the old Hannah . . .* She swallowed hard. She knew her honest answer. She knew it. But she couldn't say it.

Hannah's blue eyes pierced Jacie's. "If you knew your death would cause Solana to become a believer, would you say yes to God?"

Jacie opened her mouth, but nothing came out. Her heart pounded.

"If you knew your death was the only way Solana would come to God and spend eternity with Him, would you die?"

Jacie gulped. "No." Tears crept into her eyes. Shame filled her heart.

"Me either," Hannah said softly. She dropped the photos into the box and curled up on the bed.

"Yes, you would."

Hannah shook her head. "I've always thought I care so much about saving people. It's always been my mantra, hasn't it? 'Share the gospel to everyone everywhere.' And now I know I put limitations on God. And it makes me sick. I'm not sold out to God. I'm a phony."

Jacie's tears continued to flow. She let them. "What kind of horrible friend am I?"

Hannah scrunched a pillow fatter and propped her chin on it. "What kind of horrible friends are we both?"

"Do you think God hates us?"

Hannah shrugged, then sighed, looking away. "If we believe the Bible, we know He doesn't hate us." She paused, and then she spoke in a soft voice. "But I bet He's incredibly disappoint—"

The door flew open and Mrs. Connor appeared with a tray of warm snickerdoodle cookies and milk. "Snacks!—" She stopped and set the tray down onto Hannah's dresser.

She sat on the bed next to Hannah and began to play with her hair. "Do you want to talk?" She kindly avoided looking at Jacie's streaming face.

Hannah shrugged. Jacie bit her lip.

"Is it about Dinah?"

Hannah nodded, then said, "Sort of."

Mrs. Connor waited. The sweet snickerdoodle smell mixed in Jacie's stomach with her bitter self-loathing.

"I don't want to die," Hannah muttered into the bedclothes. "I don't care what God wants, or how much good would come out of it. I don't want to die. Not now. Not until I'm an old lady who doesn't care about life anymore."

"Who says you're going to die?" Mrs. Connor asked softly.

"Who says we're not?" Hannah retorted. Her head snapped up, her eyes filled with fire.

Jacie winced.

Mrs. Connor nodded. "True. None of us know, do we? We have to trust God with our future, no matter what that future is."

Jacie felt the words burst from within. "How can I trust God with *my* future when He stomped out Dinah and the baby's life?"

Mrs. Connor looked at Jacie. "Sometimes God has a greater purpose in our death than in our life."

"Like Rachel Scott and Cassie Bernall at Columbine, right?"

Hannah spat. She changed her tone to a holy-saccharine one. "Their deaths brought so many people to Christ. Isn't it so wonderful?"

Jacie watched, wide-eyed. She totally agreed with Hannah, but she had never seen her this way.

Mrs. Connor took a deep breath, her face taking on a sad look. "No, it wasn't wonderful that they died so young or so tragically," Mrs. Connor said calmly. "But I'm pretty amazed that God always manages to make something good come out of something bad."

"So was God powerless to stop the shooting? Was He powerless to stop Dinah from stepping onto the train car that would fall off the bridge?" Tears filled Hannah's eyes. Her voice grew soft. "I don't want to hear all your nice little answers right now, Mom, okay?"

Mrs. Connor nodded and stood. She gestured to the tray. Hannah shook her head. The tray and Mrs. Connor disappeared.

Jacie felt as though a tornado had come, rearranged her insides, and now she wasn't allowed to try to find order and put things back together. "Too many questions," she said.

"And not a single answer," Hannah replied.

chapter 8

Like a good girl, Jacie sat cross-legged on her bed dressed in her pjs and opened her Bible in front of her. She stared at the words, but they didn't seem to mean much. She knew they should, so she flipped to a different spot. She stared at the words again, and they still meant nothing. She flipped again. Nothing. What was wrong? Why did the words fall short of her heart? Instead of teaching her, or making her love God more, lately it seemed they weren't even written in English.

She let her mind take over, and her room disappeared. Like a movie playing on a screen, she could see a train car falling, falling, falling. She could hear the screams. She could see her own face in the window.

"STOP IT!" she said, smacking herself on the side of her head. "Just quit this! You're making me nuts."

She closed the Bible and crawled into bed. She lay on her back and looked through the darkness at the ceiling. "I give up," she said softly to God. "I'm not even going to try to trust You anymore. It's too hard. And look where it got Dinah. I'm done."

• • •

Jacie bounded into the cafeteria on Monday, her plans bubbling in her head.

"How was the dentist?" Becca asked her.

"Not a big deal this time. Just a teeth cleaning," Jacie said.

Solana gave a martyr's frown. "And I had to find another way to school," she said.

Tyler picked up a french fry and looked as though he might toss it at her, then changed his mind. It went into his mouth instead. "As if you had trouble finding another way to school."

"Well," Solana said, "riding with you is just not the same as coming with Jacie."

"You could have called me," Hannah said.

"And ridden on the back of the bike?" Solana gasped.

Jacie could picture Solana in her short skirt straddling the back of a bike, holding on to Hannah for dear life.

"When it's snowing I get the car," Hannah reminded her.

"Oh—" Solana said, waving her Frito in the air as if dismissing a missed opportunity.

"Where's Nate?" Jacie asked, craning her neck to look at the cafeteria line.

"Packing," Becca said.

"I thought they had movers," Hannah said.

"Nate wants to pack his own stuff." Becca rolled her eyes.

Jacie tried to sit still. But she squirmed and tried to keep her face without expression. It never seemed to work for her like it did for others.

"What's wrong with you?" Becca asked. "Need to go to the bathroom?"

"She looks like she's going to be sick," Solana said.

"No!" Jacie said, leaning forward over her lunch bag. "I have a great idea."

Hannah tilted her head like Solana's dog when you ask if she wants to go for a walk. "There's something different about you."

"She looks happy," Solana said wryly. "She's been so—"

"Shush," Jacie said. "I don't care what I've been. I've decided that if life is going to be short, then *fun* is what I want to cram my life with."

She paused and looked around the table. No one seemed to get it but Hannah, who nodded slowly, a tiny smile playing at her mouth.

"I'm the new chairman of fun around here. I've got lots of ideas, and I want us to start living it up our senior year."

"This doesn't involve alcohol, does it?" Becca asked, her eyes narrowing.

"Becca! How could you think that! Of course not!"

"I guess I—"

"No excuses. I hadn't even *thought* of that. There is so much fun to be had without mind-altering substances."

"Not according to them," Solana said, giving a quick jerk of her head toward the table next to them. It was filled with the stoners, the party kids, those who thought life could not exist without the something extra. Some of them were strung out even now.

"Look. Ignore them," Jacie said. "Ignore everything and everyone else. We're going to really take life on. We're going to experience everything we possibly can."

"Wow," Becca said. "I never thought I'd hear you say anything like that."

"The way I see it," Jacie said, "a lot of things don't have to be dangerous to be fun. There are so many things we can do. We simply need to get out there and absorb everything we can."

She looked at Tyler, who didn't seem as excited as everyone else. He had that look—the one that said he was worried about her. She'd noticed it more and more over the past couple months. She hadn't really recognized it until the year before when her car had stalled on a mountain road and everyone had been out looking for her. Tyler wore it over his entire body when he'd found her huddled underneath every item of clothing she could find in her car. She'd hoped that situation would have convinced her mother she needed a cell phone. But it didn't. They couldn't afford one. Jacie supposed they really couldn't, but she wanted one anyway.

"What's first?" Hannah asked, her eyes bright.

Jacie pulled a small, crumpled piece of paper from her jeans' back pocket. "I've got some ideas. We can vote on what's first. But I know my vote." She felt giddy, happier than she'd felt in a long time. And right now she could just flick aside that Aunt Dinah stuff like an annoying ant crawling on the back of her hand.

"We could go to the Cave of the Winds. They have an extra excursion you can pay for where they take you into some caves the general public doesn't have access to. You have to crawl through tiny tunnels. It's a four-hour adventure. Cool, huh?"

Becca stared at her. "I thought you were claustrophobic."

Jacie smiled. "It's time to get on with life, don't you think?" She looked at her list, though she didn't really need to. "Okay. Some of these things sound really stupid, but we are going to do things to revisit our childhoods. Go to the Denver Zoo. Play mini-golf. Visit all the history museums here, in Colorado Springs and Denver. We'll go to the art museum, Crazy Charlie's, Chuck E. Cheese. I've heard there's this new thing where you can create a virtual band."

"I want to be the drummer," Solana piped up.

"I'm the bass player," Hannah said to everyone's surprise. She moved her long blonde hair over one shoulder. She used to wear it only in braids or pulled up into soft bands on the back of her head making messy buns. But now she'd been wearing it down more.

"Tyler gets acoustic," Becca said.

"We can all switch off instruments," Hannah suggested.

Jacie continued. "There are a few street fairs in Denver next month. Really cool ones. Mom and I went to them last year. Lots of food, crafts, and music pavilions." She paused and looked up at them. "And then, the best thing of all is that I found a volunteer opportunity online and signed us all up."

"You signed us up without asking?" Solana asked, peeved.

"Volunteer?" Becca asked, her ears perking up.

Tyler said nothing. His worried look got worse.

"Hannah's going to really like this one," Jacie said. "We're going to clean out the attic of a very old home in Boulder."

"WHAT?" Solana said. "Have you lost your mind?"

Hannah did look interested. She leaned forward, her eyes sparkling. "Tell me more. I'm in."

"There's a huge old house where the original family and their descendants have lived for over 120 years. The last old lady died a few months ago. She had willed the house to the historical society. But it's so big, and the attic so cluttered, that they need some people to come in and catalogue items. Some of the stuff might be trash, but there might be treasures as well." Jacie smiled. "The biggest perk is that anything they plan to get rid of will be sold in some sort of estate sale. But the volunteers get the first pick of anything that doesn't have specific historical value for free."

Becca nodded. "I think I could do that."

"Do you really have time?" Solana asked.

"I keep a day open here and there for emergencies," Becca said. "Really. I've been doing much better with my time. Otis has pretty much taken over the outdoor program at the

Community Center. Both he and Mrs. R say that I am not allowed to help out that program more than once every six weeks. I've been banned from over-volunteering."

"I think it could be kind of fun," Solana conceded. "I might find some pretty funky stuff to wear."

"I just want to be in that attic," Hannah said. "I love thinking about why people save things. Touching things that were precious to someone else. It's such a mystery."

"I've got lots of other ideas, too," Jacie said. "We can celebrate the last months of our senior year, and of being together."

"Is this wise?" Tyler asked.

"What on earth are you talking about?" Becca asked. "What's not wise?"

Tyler looked down, shaking his head slowly. He looked up. "I guess I should just stay out of it."

"Stay out of what, Tyler Jennings?" Solana asked. "Quit making us crazy."

He looked at Jacie as if for approval. She shrugged. She didn't really care what he had to say.

"I don't think it's wise that we're going to ignore our big questions by having fun. We'll be stuffing what's important and hiding it behind some facade of stuff."

Hannah burst out laughing. Everyone stared at her. "And what's so bad about stuffing the questions? What's so bad about ignoring the pain? I'm so sick of myself I could scream. I do scream. I'm so tired of the questions that have no answers. I want out. And you would tell me, Tyler Jennings, that I can't take a break?"

Jacie sat up straight. Hannah has always been one to state her mind. But it used to always be something about God.

Hannah's words had a hypnotic effect. Everyone sat with wide, round eyes looking at her.

Tyler rubbed his hands together. "I told you I shouldn't say anything."

"Well, you did, Mr. Maturity," Hannah said. "So answer me."

Whoa! Jacie liked this. This new, unpredictable Hannah and this new, contemplative Tyler. How interesting.

Tyler cleared his throat. He wasn't intimidated, of that Jacie was sure. He was gathering his thoughts. Searching for the right ones, to pluck the right words from them. "It's not that I think fun is bad," he said slowly. "It's that I think Jacie is trying to run from the questions she can't answer."

"What do you suggest she do, then?" Hannah jumped in before Jacie could respond.

Tyler looked at Jacie with an expression that caught something inside her. It startled her, making her think that he was caring intensely for her. *What is wrong with my mind?* She shook her head. She was overexaggerating Tyler's expressions too much, reading into them. Still, she could sense Tyler continuing to look at her even though she'd looked away.

"I think she should face her questions head-on. Wait until they're answered." He put up his hand when Hannah opened her mouth to speak. Hannah relaxed and waited. "I don't think she should sit around and be glum all the time without doing anything fun. But I do think her reasons behind the fun are to ignore the questions. If you fill your life up with enough fun and happiness, the hard questions have no chance to get in. I don't want to see her end up ignoring the important things in life and being fake—"

"Like Jessica?" Hannah whispered softly.

Tyler caught himself and froze, as though she'd slapped him across the face. He got up from the table, swooped up his tray, unfinished burger and fries looking more like litter and less like lunch, and loped away.

The girls looked at each other. They were speechless. Jacie looked at her lap.

Hannah pursed her lips. "It just slipped out."

Becca broke the silence. "He'll get over it. That was a long time ago."

"Well, I'm not going to let him spoil my plans," Jacie said. "Give me your ideas and we'll add them to the list. Becca?"

chapter 9

Even Nora's big pink tongue and flipped-over eyelids couldn't deter Jacie's good mood. "Hi, Nora!" she sang brightly as she swept past and jogged up the stairs. "Ask your mom if you can come to art class on Thursday." Jacie unlocked the door, then glanced over her shoulder. Nora stood at the bottom of the stairs, her mouth hanging open. Jacie waited a split second before she opened the door and stepped inside. No shrieks.

Jacie dropped her stuff onto the floor. She moved through the house, running from room to room, gathering things she wanted. She paused long enough to write her mother a note, then scooped up her stuff and ran out the door.

She threw her stuff into the backseat and drove off without looking for land mines. Nothing. Maybe the trick was to catch Nora off guard.

She kept her mind on ideas and plans all the way to her art shack. Once there, she curled up on a beanbag chair—a new addition her mother found at a garage sale—and took out a sketchbook and charcoal pencil. Not to draw. To make a list. She had to plan for her Thursday class. She stared at the white page and tapped the pencil against it.

She chewed the pencil.

She tapped it.

Chewed it.

Tapped it.

Teach, she wrote.

Teach what?

She stared into the distance, hoping her brain would come up with something.

For some dumb reason, she saw the cartoon cat Garfield in her head. She drew a quick sketch of him. Then another. Then a more complicated one. Then a simple one.

That's it! she decided. She'd teach the class how to draw Garfield. The basic Garfield wasn't all that complicated. She didn't know anyone who wasn't familiar with the chubby cat. They could have fun making their own cartoons of him. She hoped Garfield's creator, Jim Davis, wouldn't mind.

Her mind tugged at her. Wanting to move her away from Garfield. So she let go. She let her hand move across the page, drawing at will. Sometimes, she just drew lines and smudged them and drew more, never really knowing what would come of it. Often nothing did. Other times, her best work happened when she let her mind go like this.

She drew and added colors, not paying full attention, just letting her mind go. Watching the light begin to dim outside her little funky shack, she used the same golden colors on paper that filtered in through the window.

It was weird to draw this way. She admitted it. How could someone not know what they were drawing until it was all over? Wasn't she the artist? How could she not know?

But she didn't. It didn't matter. Letting the lines flow was what mattered. Smudge, color, draw.

She closed her eyes for a moment's rest, then opened them.

Her happy mood sucked out of her as if someone had put a vacuum hose to her mouth and switched it on.

A train derailing, falling, making a cross with a bridge as it falls. Underneath, large, strong arms ready to catch it, cradle it as though it were falling into a pillow.

In one corner, a young pregnant woman holds open a door. Sunlight streams in. People move toward the sunlight. In the sunlight a bright figure happily hugs a woman who is joyful to be hugging him as well. A little girl looks under things, finding a cross everywhere she looks.

• • •

"Jacie."

Jacie didn't know if she wanted to talk to Tyler. What would she say? She felt cranky. She didn't want to apologize. Maybe he was going to apologize for storming off—not that he needed to.

"I'm not sorry," Tyler said as if he'd been reading her mind. "I didn't call to apologize."

Jacie held the phone to her ear. She didn't know what to say. How to answer.

"You're wrong, Jacie. You need to see that."

That made her mad. "Why do I need to see that, Tyler? And who is to say whether I'm right or wrong? Do you have a hotline to God or something? Because if you do, you can ask Him the questions He refuses to answer for me."

"Is He refusing, Jacie? Or do you not want to hear what He has to say?"

She felt slugged again. It was like the wind being knocked out of her after falling off her bike, just as she thought she was getting the hang of it.

"Look, Jacie. I'm not trying to be mean." His voice had gone as soft as melted ice cream.

"Then what do you want from me, Tyler?"

"I want you to trust that God didn't do something wrong. I want you to know that God is still trustworthy. I don't want you to walk away from Him."

"I choose what I want. If I don't think He's trustworthy anymore, then I won't say I trust Him. That's not being fake."

"I want you to be open to the questions. I don't want you to close them off. You'll lose all chance of ever finding out what God intended if you do."

"I can't take it anymore, Tyler." Her head throbbed. "I can't do it."

"You don't want to do it. You choose not to."

"So what?"

"Jacie," Tyler paused. His voice held fear. She could feel it. "Are you confusing God's will with life?"

"What are you talking about?"

"We live in a world where bad things happen. People make bad choices. Innocent people get hurt. I guess I don't think everything is caused by God. Some things happen because we live in an imperfect world."

"But He could have prevented it. He could have kept Dinah in the train car with her husband."

Tyler took a deep breath. "I know," he said softly.

"So why didn't He?"

"I can't answer that."

"Neither can I. And there's a whole lot more of those unanswerable questions where that came from. So back off! I'm sick of it."

"God doesn't stop bad things from happening. But He will teach us and strengthen us—build our character if we just give Him a chance to—"

"Tyler. ENOUGH. I don't want to hear what you think. I don't want to talk about it or think about it. I told you I'm done. When you have answers for me, then you can talk, okay? Right now fun is the only thing that will help me survive." She hung up the phone before he had a chance to respond.

The next day at school, she acted as though the conversation never happened. She could tell that Tyler hurt. But she couldn't rectify it. Not now. She was barely holding herself together. She couldn't take care of him, too.

But as the day wore on and the group of friends bantered back and forth about silly, goofy things, she felt the questions and sadness falling away. Tyler's face lifted and all was well.

That Thursday, Jacie stopped by Nora's house to see if she could come to class. But no one answered the door. She felt relieved. She hadn't really wanted her to come anyway.

Jacie set up her art classroom more simply than she had the week before. She put out lots of blank paper supplied by Mrs. R. She took pencils, crayons, and some of her precious oil pastels and put them out on the tables. She pinned large posters of Garfield on the walls. She put cutout cartoons on the tables—one at each seat. She wasn't nervous today. She had it all planned. They were going to love it.

The students trickled into the classroom. Jacie was glad to see everyone had returned, with a few new kids coming in, too.

"Take a seat, everyone," she said, feeling foolish—as though she wanted to sound like a real teacher. "Today we're going to learn how to draw."

"Good," Brenda said. "I don't wanna waste no more of my time."

Jacie had positioned herself in front of a Garfield poster when the door opened.

How she'd forgotten about Marlene, she wasn't sure. Maybe she'd hoped she wouldn't show up. But in she came, her chair pushed by her grandmother. "This time, can Marlene please do some art?" the grandmother blurted. "She was mighty disappointed that she didn't get to do anything last week."

"I wasn't sure—"

"Oh, she can do anything the others do. She's fine with that. You don't need to do something special just for her."

Jacie wanted to point out the obvious—that Marlene had no capacity to do things the way "normal" people do them. But she didn't know if it would be rude to say so in front of her. Certainly it seemed her grandmother didn't believe it.

"Just strap stuff onta here," the woman said pointing to a black strap around Marlene's left wrist. As Jacie tried to inspect the band, the woman slipped out the door.

"I don't want her here," Brenda said under her breath.

"I'm glad you're *all* here," Jacie said.

Marlene moaned loudly, startling her.

She forced a smile and continued. "Today I'm going to show you how simple it is to learn to draw a figure. We'll break it down into smaller pieces. By the end of the day you'll be drawing Garfield!" she said with a flourish, waving her hand at the wall.

But by the end of the day no one had drawn Garfield. There were only distorted bubbles, balloons, and floating grins that belonged to the Cheshire cat. Frankly, the jabs Marlene put on paper, when her spastic movements actually made contact, were arguably better art than what the others had done—but not looking remotely like Garfield.

Jacie didn't know what to do. She hadn't expected this. How hard was it, really, to do simple drawings like this? She showed them again and again how you make a circle. A triangle. An inflated D. How you put it together. She didn't know who was more frustrated—she or her students.

• • •

"Oh, forget it," Becca said that night on the phone. "You'll get it right. What did Mrs. R say?"

"She said to encourage them," Jacie said.

"Don't sound so defeated. That's good advice."

"Sure. It's great advice if you have something to encourage. But I can't encourage horrible art. That's not helpful."

"Find something good and point that out."

Jacie rolled her eyes. "There's nothing good. Really. You know me, Bec. I usually find good in things where no one else sees good."

"You're right. You do."

"So, now what?"

"Keep trying," Becca said.

So Jacie tried. She tried to figure out what she could say to be encouraging. She tried not to think about unanswered questions. She tried instead to be happy in her life. She tried to make life fun and always see things in a positive light. At school, she was witty and charming, funny and happy. She said hi to everyone, looked them in the eyes, and gave them a big smile. She brought her friends funny drawings and little gifts she found at the dollar store. She arranged fun times for them during which they laughed and teased and were everything they'd always been to each other.

At home, Jacie's mother acted increasingly weird. She went on hikes and she was constantly absent, looking for the perfect dog. As far as Jacie was concerned, the perfect dog didn't eat, shed hair, or poop.

But it obviously didn't matter what she thought, because a week later, the dog showed up with dog toys, leash, bed, food, bowls, bones, and snacks. Jacie vowed not to pay much attention to the dog. She would pretend it wasn't there.

Her name was Grace. She was sort of a collage-dog. Someone cut pieces from a magazine and stuck her together in a way that was odd, yet attractive at the same time. She had a black topcoat with a copper-brown undercoat. Her front half looked exactly like a border collie. Her back half was definitely husky with a thick tail curling up over her back.

Jacie's vow didn't last long. The little rascal managed to be so sweet that she seduced her way right into Jacie's heart. How could Jacie ignore those big, brown, trusting eyes looking up at her, pleading silently for a bit of petting. The worst was when Grace put her paw on Jacie's leg whenever Jacie sat at the computer or watched TV. The paw had pressure to it with a claw digging into Jacie's thigh. Along with the offered paw placed on Jacie's leg came a pitiful look, as if Grace couldn't live another moment without tangible love . . . preferably expressed through a walk.

Excuse me, the paw and look seemed to say. *Excuse me. Excuse me. Excuse me. Can we go for a walk now? Please? Before I perish? Excuse me?*

Sometimes Jacie obliged, and sometimes she didn't. Which probably made the problem worse. If she never took Grace for a walk, Grace might quit her pesky interruptions. But then again, knowing Grace, possibly not.

If Jacie sprawled on the floor to read or do homework, Grace curled up next to her and set her snout on the small of Jacie's back, or on her stomach. There was no doubt that Grace loved her new family—immediately.

There was no doubt Grace was her mother's dog . . . or, rather, her mother was Grace's human . . . but Grace had enough love and humility and neediness to encompass anyone who came through the front door. So Jacie reluctantly opened her heart to Grace.

chapter 10

"Jacie, we need to talk," Mrs. Noland said when Jacie got home from work.

"What did I do wrong?"

Her mother smiled. "Nothing. Why do you always think you did something wrong when I say I want to talk to you?"

Jacie shrugged. "I guess because when I was little . . ."

"Even then it wasn't that bad, was it?"

"I guess not."

Mrs. Noland sighed. "Is it because we don't talk enough?"

Jacie shook her head. "No, Mom. We talk a lot. We talk about everything. All kinds of stuff. Talking with you is almost like talking to one of my friends."

"But not quite."

"That would be too weird."

"I guess."

"So maybe when you *say* you want to talk about something I get worried."

Mrs. Noland sighed again. "Let's go sit."

Jacie curled up at one end of the slip-covered sofa. Her mom curled up at the other. For a moment, Jacie saw herself in her mom. The way they curled. How they each laid one arm across the back of the sofa, the other across their lap. The tilt of her mom's head. The way her mom bit her lower lip while trying to figure out how to say whatever it was she needed to say.

"Your dad called."

"When?"

"Today. While I was working at school."

"Is he okay?" Jacie felt worried. Her father never called her mom at work.

"He's okay." Her mom took a deep breath. "He wanted to let me know he won't be able to make it to your graduation."

Jacie couldn't respond. Maybe if she pretended she didn't hear, it wouldn't be true.

"He's going to an art show in Italy. Florence. Something he can't get out of. Everything is arranged."

"Can't someone else go?"

Her mom sighed. Her lips pinched together and she looked beyond Jacie's right ear as if the answer were written behind her. "He says no. He says this is his top artist. And that they've been working for a year on it."

"Do you believe him?" Jacie asked, anger and hurt marrying in a quick ceremony in her heart, her stomach, her head, her soul.

"I think so," her mom said in a soft voice. "I know those kinds of international events take much advance planning."

Jacie closed her eyes to block out everything else, then opened them to a world where dads don't come to daughters' high school graduations. "He didn't come to my middle school graduation either," Jacie whispered.

"I know," her mom whispered back. "He said that he's very sorry. He'd be there if he could."

The room swirled around, mixing things up. The lamp melted in with the bookshelf and the television set. The floor moved upward and became part of the chair and the table.

"I'm the senior speaker. It's an honor, isn't it?"

"Yes, it's a very high honor to be chosen to be the speaker at graduation."

Tears welled up inside Jacie's chest and overflowed through her eyes. "I want him there."

"Sweetie," Jacie's mom said, leaning across the sofa and putting her hand on Jacie's arm. "It might be okay without him there."

Jacie looked at her mom, who was all blurry. "And it might not," she said, her voice barely coming out.

"I know."

Jacie's tears became a flood. And the flood became all-out sobs. Her mom crossed the gap in the sofa and pulled her daughter close. And Jacie cried and cried.

● ● ●

Dear Diary,

Jacie felt weird writing that. But she wanted to write to somebody. She wanted to talk directly to someone. But who?

Is that why people started writing Dear Diary? Just so it felt like they were writing to a person rather than to nobody?

She tapped the pen on the paper and stared at it. She wanted someone to understand her. She'd burnt out her friends. She didn't want someone to agree or disagree—she only wanted them to listen.

A name popped into her mind. She crumpled the paper in front of her and began a new one.

Dear Damien,

I know it's silly that I'm writing to you when I could just find you at lunch and talk. But I think I need to write. I really need to draw, but the drawings are so frightening that I'm afraid to try. Remember the painting I did of you? That's how my drawings are coming out now. And it scares me.

You know about death. You know it too well. But what about the death of a dream? Or death of an expectation? Or how about just too many things happening at once?

The love of Solana's life has gone off to college, Becca hurt her leg so she's ineligible for college scholarships, Tyler didn't get into CU Boulder, Nate has to move far away, my dad is too busy with work to come see me graduate. I know, none of those things really matter when we're talking about life and death. And there's too much death, too—wonderful, pregnant Aunt Dinah dies in a tragic accident, and that little boy you—I'm sorry. I shouldn't mention that, should I?

But, Damien, I don't know what to do. I don't know how to handle all these hard things. I can't go to God with them because—well, He could have changed the outcome of any of these things, couldn't He? So how can I go to the One who could have worked these things out, and didn't?

Do you understand God? Can you explain Him to me?

Of course you can't. I'm not sure I can respond to my questions by becoming "bad" like you did.

So what do I do? How do I gather all these hard things and still face life with a genuine good attitude?

Jacie

● ● ●

Jacie showed up at Nate's going away party wearing a stylish skirt, a darling blouse, sandals, and a smile.

"It's freezing out there," Mrs. McKinnon said when she opened the front door. "Did you forget?"

"Yes it's freezing," Jacie said walking past her, holding the plate of peanut butter cookies she and her mom had baked that afternoon. "But I knew I'd be inside where it's warm."

Mrs. McKinnon leaned forward and whispered, "You look awfully darling."

Jacie smiled—a real smile—and whispered back, "Thanks. That was the point I hoped to make."

Mrs. McKinnon stood up straight. "And whom are you hoping to make it for?"

Jacie tilted her head. "You don't know?"

Mrs. McKinnon raised her eyebrows—just like Becca when she realized something she'd been missing. "I . . . really? I mean, I have an idea, but—"

Jacie just grinned, saying nothing else.

"Everyone is in the basement."

"Food, too?"

"Food, too. Take your cookies with you."

Jacie went down the wide, carpeted stairs to the fully outfitted basement. Crowds of kids from Stony Brook High stood in their usual clumps. They chattered over the booming music. A few looked up as she came down the stairs. "Hey, Jacie!" they called.

She waved her free hand. "Where's the guest of honor?" she asked Kara.

Kara leaned forward so Jacie could hear her over the din. "He and Becca are off in the ping-pong room moping. I swear. What good is a party if you can't have fun?" She turned back to her group and dove into the conversation.

Jacie shook her head. *Duh*, she thought. *Wow, I wonder why Nate would be sad? Maybe because he's leaving his school and his girlfriend in the final half of his senior year?*

She left the frivolity in the main room for the dismal sadness in the other. A couple of big guys from the basketball team bounced around at either end of the ping-pong table trying to slaughter each other in the game. Jacie wondered how many ping-pong balls they'd flattened in the process.

"Jacie," Hannah said from the far end of the room. Hannah moved toward her, took her arm, and pulled her in.

"Peanut butter cookies anyone?" Jacie asked lamely of the morose group huddled there.

"Hi," everyone said.

"Put them on the table with the others." Becca waved her hand toward the happy room. Her eyes looked red and swollen from crying.

Jacie set the plate on a small side table. "Hi, Nate," she said. She walked to him to give him a quick hug. Instead, he pulled her in and hugged her like they'd been best friends and would never see each other again. Well, half of that was accurate.

When he finally let go, she noticed Tyler looking at the ping-pong game, obviously not really watching it. It looked more like he was looking at her, but pretending not to. She gave him a shy smile. His return smile melted her.

"Damien's here," Solana said. "He wants to talk to you."

"Okay," Jacie said.

Tyler said nothing.

Jacie wondered what was going on inside that head of his. He looked like he wanted to talk. She waited a moment, giving him a chance to say something. Since he kept silent, she picked up her plate of cookies and went into the noisy room. She moved through the kids to the counter where she uncovered her cookies and set the plate amongst all the other goodies. A large note posted above the treats said, "Don't forget to sign Nate's good-bye card!" with an arrow pointed to a table against the wall.

Jacie wandered over to the card, saying happy hellos to everyone she passed. She surveyed the array of felt pens, chose a few, and drew a quick picture of Nate and Becca, and a few faces behind them—obviously Tyler, Hannah, Solana, and herself. She couldn't figure out what to write. "Gone, but not forgotten," sounded hokey. "We all love you and will miss you," sounded too general.

"Can't think of anything to say?"

She stood up and turned around to face Damien. She flushed. She'd written that note, but hadn't given it to him. She didn't even know if she would. She was afraid it might open things between them in a way best left closed.

His scent surrounded her. She wanted to close her eyes and drink it in, remembering their kisses—had it been over a year ago? She forced herself to keep her eyes open and her smile simple. She shook her head. "No, I can't. What words are there?"

Why is it that a former boyfriend can still have an effect even when you don't want him to? It's not fair.

"I haven't signed yet because I couldn't think of anything, either."

"You guys didn't hang out much, did you?"

"No. But Nate is the kind of guy who just fits in everywhere. Friendly to everyone. He and Becca always took time to talk to me." He shrugged. "Not everyone was willing to talk to the 'bad boy.' "

Jacie tilted her head and put the cap on her pen. "But you're not the 'bad boy' anymore."

Damien's green eyes stared into hers. "Not everyone is willing to see that." He shrugged.

"Am I?" Jacie blurted, wishing she hadn't.

Damien smiled and nodded. "Definitely. More than most people I know. You are accepting. Forgiving."

His word stabbed her. *Forgiving?* She felt her cheeks grow warm again. Was she forgiving her father for not putting her first in his life? Was she forgiving God for killing Aunt Dinah? She suddenly realized she was shaking her head. "No."

"Yes, you are," Damien said.

"I used to be," she answered. "Maybe some things are too big to be forgiven."

Damien shook his head. "You forgave me. You accepted me. You saw past what I'd done. You gave me hope that not everyone would hate me, that I could forgive myself and forgive God for letting that little boy die. You showed me that my mistake shouldn't end my life . . ." His voice trailed off.

Jacie knew that if he'd finished the sentence, he might have said, ". . . even though it ended someone else's."

"You were willing to let me change," he said quickly, filling the gap. "I appreciate that."

"You're welcome," she said, wanting to avoid where the

conversation could go. Or where her thoughts probably should go—that she should allow others the freedom to be themselves, flaws and all. Right now she wanted to be mad at her dad and God. She especially didn't want to allow God freedom in her life. That was too terrifying.

"You wanted to see me?" Jacie said, threading the pen through her fingers.

Damien shrugged. "Nothing special. We don't see each other at school much anymore. I just wondered how you're doing, how your speech preparation is coming, if you have a date to the prom, all that stuff."

Jacie felt a funny slug to her chest. Was he asking her to the prom? Or was he just interested in her life? "I'm doing fine," she lied. At that moment she knew she wouldn't give him the letter she'd written. She'd keep it in her journal, the questions unasked. "My speech isn't coming along very well. I guess I have speech-writer's block. And yes, I do have a date for the prom. Do you?"

"Not yet," Damien said, looking a little less happy than he had a split second before. "Who are you going with?"

"Tyler," Jacie said. "He's taking all of us."

"All of you?"

Jacie smiled. "Solana, Becca, Hannah, and me."

He looked surprised. "Well! There go all the best choices."

Jacie slugged him playfully. "Aww. You always were such a flatterer."

"Hey. I only tell the truth. And Tyler's the luckiest guy in school."

"Damien," a girl called coming toward them. "Play pool with me."

Damien put up his hand. "In a sec, Robin." He turned to Jacie. He leaned forward so he didn't have to shout. "Never forget who you are, Jacie."

He walked away before she could ask him to explain. *Who am I?* She'd like to know what she wasn't supposed to forget.

She uncapped the pen and stole Damien's words. "Nate. Never forget who you are—an official member of the *Brio* gang."

chapter 11

"This one is *darling*," Solana crowed, holding up a bright red strapless gown. She viewed it from all sides. "Way too darling." She threw it over her arm with the 10 other *darling* dresses she'd found.

"Dillard's on a Sunday afternoon in spring," Jacie said, eyeing all the gowns on the "50-75% Off" rack. "*The* place to find prom dresses."

Becca frowned at one she'd pulled off the rack. "I don't know, I just don't know," she said. "They're all so . . . so . . ."

"Skimpy?" Hannah asked.

"Feminine," Solana replied for Becca without looking up.

Becca shoved the dress onto the crowded rack. "These so aren't me," she complained.

"Me either," Hannah said, frowning at a backless.

"We all have to blend," Solana said.

Without looking at her, Jacie knew Becca was rolling her eyes. "Who cares if we blend?" Becca asked.

"Because we're all going together," Solana said. "So we all have to look hot together."

"You can't be hot in any of these skimpy things," Hannah complained.

"I meant *hot* as in—"

"I *know* what you meant," Hannah said, smiling. "I'm *teasing*. You do know what teasing is, don't you?"

"I do, but I hear it so rarely from you," Solana said, obviously in a funk about missing the tease.

"I found one for you," Jacie said, taking a black gown from the rack and handing it to Hannah. "It's classic without being too *sexy*."

Hannah eyed it warily. "I guess I could try it on."

"Here's a blue one," Becca said, shoving a sky blue dress her way.

"Hold the phone," Solana said, using some archaic expression they'd just heard on an old movie the night before. "I've found it."

Hannah looked at the corset and skirt. "I can't—"

"Oh, but you *can*," Jacie said. "It's perfect with your hair—especially if you wear it down. And we can find a thin blouse to go under the corset."

Becca nodded emphatically. "You will look gorgeous—"

"Without being too, too—" Hannah couldn't say it.

"Yes, Hannah," Solana said, sounding a bit frustrated. "Without being too sexy."

Jacie abandoned them for a nearby department and found three white blouses that just might work with the corset. She wanted Hannah to feel comfortable. It was going to be hard enough for her to go to a dance without wearing a dress that would make her want to hide.

"Try these," she said to Hannah, handing over the blouses.

Hannah disappeared into the dressing room area. Solana followed with her stack of dresses.

"I'll never find anything," Becca complained.

"Because you don't want to," Jacie told her.

"Yes, I do," Becca insisted.

"No, you don't," Jacie said gently. "You don't want to go if Nate can't go."

Instantly tears welled up in Becca's eyes. "It's not fair, Jacie. It's bad enough he had to move, without moving before graduation."

"Not much seems fair lately," Jacie agreed. Her questions about God's goodness threatened to swarm in, but pictures of the fun she insisted they focus on derailed the questions. She felt more confused than ever.

She slid hangers on the rod without really looking at the dresses. But then, one caught her eye. "Would you be willing to try this one on?"

Becca looked at it. For a moment it seemed her eyes lit up, then a bleakness came in again. "I guess."

They joined the others in the largest dressing room, hoping no one in a wheelchair would appear right when they all had their clothes off. They giggled and tried on dresses, Solana trying on the conservative ones, Hannah trying on the daring ones, Becca trying on the feminine ones, and Jacie trying on just about everything. They laughed at how the dresses hung on one, and barely fit another.

In the midst of it, Jacie imagined Tyler and blushed.

• • •

"Mom!" Jacie called as she entered the front door. "I found it!" She brought in the swishy bag behind her, holding it up high so the knotted bottom didn't touch the ground. "It's perfect—well, not as perfect as the homecoming dress, but it's great and it only cost $40!"

Her mom appeared at the top of the stairs, wearing her nice black trousers and a cream turtleneck sweater. "Oh, let me see!"

"Are you going somewhere?" Jacie asked, feeling left out.

"Why, yes." Her mother came down the stairs. Jacie could swear her face had turned a bit red.

"You didn't tell me—"

"It's kind of a last-minute thing. There's leftover casserole in the refrigerator, or you can scrounge for what you want."

Jacie just stared at her, all kinds of feelings roiling inside. She felt so incredibly selfish. But wasn't Mom supposed to always be there? Wasn't Mom supposed to always be at home when she wasn't at work? Well, maybe she could go to the grocery store. "Where are you going?"

"Out to dinner. To a movie."

"Can I come?"

Her mom looked at her. She shifted her weight, then walked swiftly to get her coat. "Not this time."

"Who are you going with?"

"Rich."

"Who?"

"A man, Jacie. We met on the Saturday hike."

"You didn't tell me you met anyone." Jacie thought her heart would flutter to a stop.

Her mom shrugged. "I didn't think it was any big deal."

"He's asking you out on a *date* and it's no big deal?"

"I didn't know he was going to ask me out, Jacie. We just talked on the hike. I thought he was nice. I guess he thinks I'm nice too." She picked up her purse and clutched it tightly.

"Is he a Christian?"

"Yes. That's what we talked most about. Faith. Church. Life. God."

"Pretty intense for a hike, isn't it?" Jacie could feel her bratty self coming out. But she didn't really care. Her mom going on a *date*? What was next? She shuddered to think about it.

Her mom crossed her arms, the purse strap dangling over one of them. "You know I tend to avoid people who only talk about surface things. I *like* talking about intense things—on a hike or anywhere else."

"You don't talk about intense things with me. Like I had no idea this surface thing of meeting some guy on a hike had even happened."

"No, Jace. We don't talk on a deep level very often. You don't seem to want to."

Jacie felt her own cheeks grow warm. Her mom was right. But Jacie wasn't about to admit it. They talked a lot—but mostly about Jacie's stuff. Never about really deep or important things pertaining to her mother. She clenched her teeth and didn't know what to say.

"Show me your dress," her mom said, "and then I have to get going."

Jacie unknotted the bag and shimmied the plastic over the top of the hanger.

Jacie's mom dropped the purse and coat onto the sofa. "It's gorgeous. You'll look so pretty in this. Where did you ever find this copper color? It's going to look fabulous against your skin."

"Thanks," Jacie said. But the normal glow she would have felt after her mother's gushing words wasn't there. It was eclipsed by her mother going on a *date*. She felt like she could spit the word.

"Good night, Jace," her mom said as she lightly kissed her cheek. "I'll be home later."

Jacie could only nod. The moment her mom was out the door she called Becca. Solana answered the phone. "What do you want?" Solana asked. "We just spent all day together.

Haven't you had enough of me? I s'pose not. I *am* hard to resist."

"What are you doing answering Becca's phone?" Jacie asked.

"Becca's mom saw on caller ID that it was you. They don't want my help fixing dinner, so they asked me to get it." Solana must have popped something into her mouth. Her words were now a bit muffled. "So? Whaw oo whan?"

"My mom is going out on a *date*!"

"Really?" Solana's voice grew faint as she turned to yell to the others in the room. "Jacie's mom went out on a date!" She turned back to the phone. "What's his name? Who is he? Where'd she meet him?"

Jacie didn't want to tell her all that stuff. She didn't want it to be real. "Look, Sol. I don't think it's such a good idea."

"Is that such a horrible thing?"

"Yes! Why can't she just forget about men? Why can't she just stay single? Things have been going along great."

"You just want her to be at your beck and call."

Jacie bit the inside of her cheek. Was that true? Of course it wasn't! The truth was that mothers had no business dating.

Solana piped up. "I could loan her my leopard mini—"

Jacie cut Solana off with sharp words. "Mom is all I've ever had."

"And she's sacrificed so much for you. Isn't it time to let her have a life? Otherwise, she'll have nothing when you go away to school."

"Where's Tyler?" Jacie had no idea why she asked or what she'd say to him.

"I think he's busy on Becca's computer looking up the *Homestarrunner Daily*."

"Why are all of you over there anyway?" Jacie asked, feeling hurt she hadn't been invited.

"Hannah's not here. We dropped her off on the way home."

"When did Tyler go over there?"

"His computer isn't working. Or maybe his dad won't let him use the computer. I can't remember which."

"And he had to come over just to look up *Homestarrunner*?" Jacie felt extremely agitated.

"No. He came over to do his homework. But you know what always comes first."

Jacie put her head in her hands. She took a deep breath. Emotions were trampling all over her like an outraged herd of elephants. She couldn't figure out which one was smashing on her next.

"Jace?"

"Yeah, Sol. I think I need to go work on my lesson for next week's art class."

"Okay! But you know you can come over. Mrs. McKinnon said she can pretend today is a Friday. Mr. M is off on some trip. And Alvaro is clomping around on his stick horse. Kassy is off at some friend's house."

"No thanks," Jacie said, wanting very much to go over. But she knew she'd be horrible company for anyone. Anyone except Hannah.

"If you're looking for fun, this is the place," Solana said. "But if you're looking for sympathy, we're all sold out here."

Jacie wondered why Solana suddenly sounded like Jack Nicholson.

After saying good-bye, she clicked off the phone. She ran upstairs to hang up her dress, then traipsed back downstairs and flipped through her mom's DVD collection—which seemed to be growing rapidly. "Where's she getting the money for these?" she asked Grace. Lately she'd been talking to the dog as if she were a person. She flipped through the titles: *Anywhere but Here*, *Princess Diaries*, *Steel Magnolias*, *Freaky Friday*, *Not Without*

My Daughter. Jacie flipped through them again, realizing that each of the movies was about mothers and daughters. Mothers and daughters growing up in some ways together.

Come to think of it, one of these movies was always playing when Jacie got home. Her mom wasn't actually watching the movies. It was as though she put on movies the way most people put on music. The weirdest thing was, no matter where her mom was in the house, she always seemed to be wiping her eyes when Jacie came into the room. But Jacie hadn't let the fact soak in before now. She'd kind of written it off to whatever cleaning stuff or whatever vegetable she chopped creating a little bit of moisture in her eyes.

Was she crying?

How stupid can I get?

Jacie grabbed a movie and jammed it into the DVD player. She popped some kettle corn in the microwave. She flopped onto the floor with some huge pillows and pulled a blanket over her. Grace lumbered over, snuffled the blanket, turned three circles, then flopped next to her. Jacie took the first bite of hot, sweet popcorn and pointed the remote. She was going to have fun. She was going to enjoy life. She was going to stop feeling as though everything she'd ever known or understood were a pool of melting butter under the heat of life.

chapter 12

"How was your mom's date?" Solana asked at school the next day. She wiggled her eyebrow a couple times.

Jacie stared at her juice box, wishing her eyes could pierce it through with angry fire. She hated it and everything else. She did not feel like being coy and cute about her *mother* dating like a teenager.

Solana tilted her head and drew closer to Jacie's face, peering up into it. "Come on. You're not going to deny us the interesting stuff, are you?"

Jacie took some deep breaths. "Do we have to talk about this?"

Becca nodded her head, her mouth full of sandwich. "Umm-hmm."

Hannah gave a distant smile. She had opened her sandwich and was eating each layer by itself—bread, meat, lettuce. Now she was working on a tomato.

"I think we should talk about the way Hannah is eating her sandwich," Jacie said.

Becca and Solana looked at each other as if considering this.

"Naw," Solana said a moment later.

"Help me here, Hannah," Jacie pleaded.

Hannah smiled. "I agree with them. Your mother's date is far more interesting than me dissecting a sandwich."

Tyler sauntered up and sat on the table. "How was your mom's date? I'm sure you spilled it already, but hey. Spill again."

"She won't tell," Becca said with an exaggerated pout. A slow smile spread across her face. "Shall we make her?"

Jacie looked from one to the other. "You *wouldn't*."

Before she could extract herself from the lunch bench, the others had pounced. She shrieked as they tickled her. "Okay! Okay!" she gasped through giggles. "Stop! I'll tell. I promise."

The horde backed off, their faces eager.

Jacie considered a quick escape, but thought better of it. They'd tackle her in the cafeteria. It wouldn't be a pretty sight. "Well," she said brightly, as if beginning a very exciting tale. "She was gone for a long time. When she came home she said—" She paused to draw out their anticipation. Solana was nearly leaning into her lunch.

"Good night." Jacie picked up her sandwich and took an enormous bite.

"NO," Solana demanded. "You can't leave us stranded here. Details. Was her lipstick smeared?"

"She doesn't wear lipstick," Jacie mumbled around the mouthful.

"Was she smiling?" Hannah asked.

Jacie felt her stomach clench. She'd been beaming. Jacie had wondered if she'd ever seen her mother like that before. "Yeah," Jacie said softly. "She was."

"What did she say about him?" Becca probed.

"Fine." Jacie realized they wouldn't quit until they believed she'd told them every shred. "She came in and smiled. I didn't really want to know how it was. I was still mad that she'd gone out on a date. And I'd watched one of her dumb movies, and that put me in a worse mood."

"Which one?" Becca asked.

"*Freaky Friday*."

"Ooooh," Hannah said. "I'm so sorry."

Becca nodded.

"I haven't seen that one," Tyler said. "What's wrong with it?"

"Single mom gets remarried," Solana said.

"Big mistake," Tyler said.

"You're tellin' me," Jacie said.

"Get on with the story," Hannah said, leaning over the last layer of her sandwich—bread covered with mayonnaise.

"Hannah!" Solana said. "You've got to stop hanging around me, girl. I'm obviously a bad influence."

"Hush," Hannah said, not taking her eyes off Jacie.

Jacie could see it all in her head, like a movie. "She sat on the edge of the easy chair and just looked at me. I figured I should be polite. 'Well?' I asked. 'How was it?'

" 'He seems really nice,' she said. I swear she looked like Solana after she's seen a new guy."

"Impressive," Solana said.

"Then she just looked at me with that goofy grin. So I had to ask." Jacie's friends looked like vultures waiting for an animal to die.

" 'Where'd you go? What'd you see?' She said they went to this new restaurant called The Elephant Bar. African theme or something. She said they talked so long they almost missed the movie. Rich told her talking is important, but so is just relaxing together."

"How sweet," Hannah said.

Jacie rolled her eyes. "Then they went to some artsy movie I hadn't heard of."

"At Kimball's?" Hannah asked.

"You know about Kimball's?" Solana asked.

"Of course. My parents love some of the movies they show there."

"And then?" Becca asked.

"They went to coffee and lived happily ever after," offered Tyler.

Jacie thought it weird how much Tyler seemed to be enjoying this.

"Not quite," Jacie said. "But they did go to coffee and talked forever until Mom told him she had to get home."

"Ahh," Becca said. "I'll have to e-mail Nate. Love is on the horizon."

"Whoa! Slow down," Jacie protested. "We're talking *one* date. She doesn't know this guy. He could be a total jerk. A closet lunatic. Mass murderer. *Anything*."

"Or the nicest thing that's happened to her in a long time," Hannah said.

Everyone looked at her, astonished.

"Hannah, they aren't courting," Solana reminded her.

Hannah rolled her eyes. "Courtship is for kids. She's an adult. She can make her own decisions. It's between her and God and her friends to hold her accountable."

"You don't think it's wrong?" Becca asked.

"No, I don't. I'm glad to see something nice happen to somebody for a change."

Becca made a "well-I-hadn't-thought-of-that" face.

"It is nice," Tyler said. "Has your mom dated before?"

"Not that I know of," Jacie said. "I don't want to think she could have done this a lot."

Solana shook her head vigorously. "No way. She's acting too geeky for someone who's used to this."

Jacie pondered her juice box. She squeezed it too hard, and some grape juice squirted a purple stream into her open bag of Cool Ranch Doritos.

"Do you think your mom will get married?" Hannah asked.

"Of course she will," Solana said.

Jacie shrugged. She hated the thought. She had that same feeling she'd felt when her mom got all excited to see Grace at the end of every day. *Jealousy*.

"It would be hard for you, wouldn't it?" Tyler asked, his caring eyes boring into hers.

"Well!" Solana said. "Look who's decided to become Mr. Compassion."

Tyler turned red and looked away. Jacie felt a link to understanding ripped from her.

"Life goes on," Hannah chirped sounding terribly insincere. "We just get on with it, don't we?"

"You were right," Becca said, obviously changing the subject. "It's nice to see something good happening to somebody."

"Something good is happening to all of us," Hannah continued in the mocking voice. "We just can't see it right now."

"Who are you quoting?" Solana asked, stuffing the last of a cookie into her mouth.

Hannah looked at her squarely. "All the wonderful people at church who are sure they understand exactly what God has intended for everyone in the world."

"Good!" Jacie said. "Maybe they can tell me what God has planned for my future."

"Mine too," Tyler added.

Solana sat agape. "Hannah is ripping on the church people?"

Hannah sighed. "I don't mean to sound like everyone is heartless. There are so many people who have just come up to hug me. Or to say they don't understand. There are only a few who say really stupid things like 'God needed her more than you did.' Or 'Your aunt is in a better place.' The worst is when people tell me that this whole thing is God's best. If this is God's best, then what's His worst?"

"Have we ever said stuff like that?" Becca asked.

Hannah shook her head. "No, I did. But now I'm with Jacie. This stuff keeps coming up, but I don't want to keep thinking about it." She looked at Jacie. "What's our fun this week?"

"Did you forget?" Solana asked. "The attic. Dark. Full of ghosts of the past."

Becca rolled her eyes. "We don't believe in ghosts."

Solana shook her head. "Not *that* kind of ghost. It's just a word for things that hang around. Not real beings that float around."

"Pieces of people's lives," Hannah said. "Parts of themselves they left behind. Those kinds of ghosts, right?"

Solana stared at her. "You're scaring me more all the time, H. I don't like that you're starting to understand me."

Hannah shrugged and smiled. "Maybe I'm the one who should be scared."

chapter 13

Jacie followed Tyler up the narrow steps inside the giant old house. Solana had the lead, practically bounding up into the black unknown, her shoes clomping the floor loudly enough to wake the dead. Becca took the stairs two at a time behind her, her boots making an even louder pounding noise. Then Tyler, Jacie, and Hannah brought up the rear. Jacie's face was at the unfortunate level of Tyler's behind. She lagged a bit to create some distance. But then Hannah's face was at her behind.

Bodies are so weird, Jacie thought, and her mind automatically switched to artist mode. Now instead of Tyler's behind, she saw his blue jeans in form and contrast. Faded here. Dirt smudged there. Probably hand-shaped from his wiping off something. *Why don't guys ever use towels?* Could she capture that detailed weave in the denim? The dirt smudges would be easy. But the blue-and-white threads, with the blue shifting color along each thread—

Solana threw open the door at the top of the stairs. It

banged against the wall, then started to swing shut. She fastened the door to the eyelet in the wall with a dangling metal hook. She disappeared into the darkness. A light flicked on, the brightness spilling into the stairwell. "Wow!"

Becca disappeared into the light. "Whoa! Lookit this."

Tyler turned the corner, then Jacie.

The pitched roof covered a large room filled with boxes and furniture and dust and *stuff*. Stuff everywhere.

"Do we have to get all this done today?" Solana asked, slowly turning to take it all in.

Jacie looked around the room. Beyond some of the stacks were other doors. Shelves. Alcoves. Everywhere she looked, there was stuff. She didn't know what else to call it. "No. We can put in as much time as we want. If we want to come back later, we can. They'll find someone else when we're done."

Hannah hugged herself and shivered.

"Ghosts?" Solana teased.

Hannah shook her head. "It's wonderful to be in a place that holds so much history. So much life."

"Seems to me like it's more about death," Solana said.

"No," Hannah said emphatically. "It's all about life. What was important to the people who lived here. What they hoped for."

"Who they were," Becca said. She'd flipped open a box lid and had removed some sort of yearbook from 1949. She had it opened to the first page where handwriting scrawled diagonally up the side of the page. "Listen to this."

Theresa,

I can't find the words to tell you how much your friendship has meant to me. I am so, so glad I met you. Your strong faith inspired my days. I'm a better person for having known you. I love you so much.

Dianne

Jacie looked at the old book. *Would anyone write such kind things about her in her yearbook?*

"Makes you wish you knew Theresa, doesn't it?" Becca asked.

"I probably wouldn't have liked her," Solana said. "Too saccharine."

"You don't think anyone would write stuff like that in your yearbook?" Tyler asked.

"No."

"I would," Hannah said, ending the discussion. "Not the faith part, of course. But you've had faith in your friends. And you have been a really good friend to me."

"Huh, yeah." Solana turned away, but not before Jacie saw her blush.

Tyler had taken a box from the top of a stack. DIARIES was printed on the side. "Here's some juicy reading."

Jacie waited for Hannah to complain or protest. But she didn't.

He dug out a small book, letting it fall open, and began to read:

> *I am so angry at Paul. I'm tired of him running off when we have a fight, leaving me with the kids. They all seem to know something's wrong and the moment he leaves in a huff, they all start screaming. Jimmy beats Patsy over the head with her favorite doll. Timmy and Mindy start arguing about anything and everything, usually what belongs to who. I swear the poor dog is going to die of fright one of these days. She hightails it for behind the sofa and sits back there shivering until I rescue her. "Sweetie," I call. But it's as if she doesn't know her own name. I honestly don't think I can take it much longer.*

Jacie walked around the room as Tyler read, looking at things. Right away she could see things that could be sold. Empty picture frames, some with the glass broken, hopeful to be replaced and made new.

"Look," she said, pointing to a worn leash. It hung next to a photo of a small black-and-white dog. Maybe a Jack Russell terrier. A tiny paw print in plaster sat beside it. "Do you think this was Sweetie?"

Hannah came and looked closely. She picked up the paw print and turned it over. "Sweetie" it said in a child's awkward printing.

Tyler read from a different day. "Hey. Listen to Valentine's Day the same year."

> *Paul is so wonderful to me. How did I get such a marvelous husband? I woke to breakfast in bed. An hour later the florist arrived with a dozen long-stemmed red roses. Tonight he plans to take me to our favorite restaurant in Bear Creek. I told him we can't afford it. He says I'm worth it. He even hired a babysitter. But more than those outward things, he shows me he loves me almost every day. He talks to me. He listens to me. My goodness, he even listens to my endless stories about the children. Whether they're good and darling or the cause of insanity, he listens. He encourages me to be all that I want to be. My biggest Valentine's gift is that he signed me up for a writing class. Everyone else thinks I'm being frivolous and flighty. After all, a woman's place is in her home with her family—and nowhere else. Paul understands that I need more than that.*

"I guess Paul is redeemed," Tyler proclaimed as if it were himself who had been absolved of all guilt.

"I suppose we should start sorting." Becca replaced the yearbook, sighing. "I'd much rather scoop up the memories and try to picture who these people were."

"We still can," Hannah said. She turned to Jacie. "Didn't the organizers say we could keep anything we want?"

Jacie nodded. "As long as it's not of historical value."

"Do you think the journals and the yearbooks have historical value?" Hannah asked.

"We could put them aside and see," Jacie said.

"I would think it depends on how famous this family was," Solana said, "and if the journals contain anything that relates to major historical events."

"We'll just have to read them and find out," Jacie said.

Tyler offered to go downstairs and bring up the flattened boxes they'd brought with them.

While he was gone, the girls began to walk through the entire attic to get an idea of the scope of their mission.

"One room entirely filled with chairs and other old furniture," Solana called out. "Looks like a mishmash of antiques and old junk pieces."

"Shelves and shelves of boxes," Hannah called out. "If they're labeled right, there's all kinds of old camera equipment."

"This seems like the book room," Jacie said. "Bookshelves and boxes full of them." She twitched her nose, then rubbed it. It didn't help. An enormous sneeze blew through.

"Bless you!" Becca called.

"Wow," Hannah said. "You should see some of these old photos. Denver when there wasn't much to it. Boulder way back."

"I think we should start here," Becca called from the main room. "Look at all this cool stuff."

"I want these cameras!" Hannah wailed. "An old Brownie. Box cameras of all shapes and sizes. Cameras from every era.

And it looks like they were still functional when they were stored. Whoever packed them wrote instructions for using them."

"What are you so upset about?" Solana said, dusting her hands off on her pants. "See if they'll give you one."

"They won't let us have these kinds of things," Hannah explained. "But boy, I'd love to keep some."

"You never know," Tyler said, dumping the flattened cardboard onto the main floor near Becca. "Some of the cameras might be easy to come by."

For the next few hours they laughed and sneezed and sorted and gasped. "Why in the world would someone save *this*?" Becca asked holding up a rusty cheese grater.

"They knew Hannah was coming," Tyler said. "She only takes marriage proposals that involve cheese."

"Hah-hah," Hannah said. In Venezuela on their mission trip the past summer, she'd accidentally told a man jabbering in Spanish that she'd marry him for a piece of cheese.

"Oooh," Solana said, holding up a musty party dress. "Bet I'd look hot in this."

"Yeah. If you lived in the '50s," Becca said.

"I look hot in anything," Solana protested.

"Especially in the summer," Hannah quipped.

"Then how about this?" Tyler tossed her a nearly new apron with the blackened shape of an iron burned into it.

"Where'd you find that?" Jacie asked.

"Stuffed behind a drawer in this dresser," he said, motioning to the beaten bureau behind him.

"Why would anyone save that?" Becca asked.

"It wasn't saved," Hannah told them. "It was hidden."

"You think one of the kids was supposed to iron it?" Jacie asked.

"And got sidetracked," Becca added.

"By some boy," Hannah said. "She let him kiss her and while he did, she left the iron sitting on the apron. When she stopped kissing him, she knew she'd be in trouble if she didn't hide the evidence."

"Hannah!" Solana said. "My, but you have a racy imagination."

"I learned everything I know from you," she said sweetly. She made little kissy noises at her.

Jacie expected a snide comment and was surprised when Solana made kissy noises back.

The more boxes or drawers they opened, the faster they got at evaluating the item and deciding where it should go. Fund-raiser sale. Goodwill clothes. Possible antique clothing. Items to be decided upon by the Historical Society. Trash.

Jacie opened box after box, forgetting about her dirty hands. She dug through each box, excited to see what was in each one.

Sometimes the items tugged at her heart: a tiny dress and shoes, a baby nightgown still smelling of babyness, a stuffed animal worn through with love. At first she read all the school papers of the children who had once lived in this house. But soon, she scanned them quickly, tossing most of them into the trash box.

She wondered why it hurt to do that. Did she feel she was ending someone's life? The only proof of their existence? Her thoughts continued to draw her, to pull her in a direction she did not want to go.

"Attics are wonderful storehouses of memories treasured and valued," Hannah said. "Or they could be reminders that we are all terminal. How terminal, no one knows. Our existence could be reduced to papers, old worn-out toys, evidence of our mistakes, and rusty kitchen utensils."

"Okay," Solana said, holding up clothes to herself and then away from herself, trying to judge their age and importance.

"Enough with the philosophy. Isn't this supposed to be a fun day?"

"Yeah," Becca said to Hannah. "Write a report. But leave us out of it!"

"I wish they had an old guitar around here," Tyler said.

"I wish they had oil paints and brushes," Jacie said. "Or some old artwork someone in the house drew."

"Speaking of which," Hannah said, an old shoebox in her lap, the dusty lid on the floor beside her, "look at this." She stared at a blue piece of notepaper. She stared as if it had the mystery of the universe written there.

Solana looked at it over her shoulder and stared. She looked like she was going to say something sassy, but stopped.

Becca crawled across a pile of old clothing until her chin rested on Hannah's knee. "Wow."

Hannah leaned over Becca and handed it to Tyler. "Give this to Jacie."

Tyler looked at it and cocked his head like a dog trying to understand what the humans were saying. He handed it to Jacie without comment.

The caption, written in an adult hand, said, "GOD, by Ethel, age 3."

Ethel had scribbled her version of God. Round scribbles rose up from the floor of the paper into its sky. Bigger the circles grew. Rippling bubbles collided and intersected, wild, and yet with a sort of form. There was something about the scribbling that looked remarkably like—well, like something. Power. Strength. Untamed. Creativity come to life.

Jacie looked at it, then felt it with her fingers. *Why did it affect them all so much?*

"If you could draw God," Hannah said softly, "would He look like that?"

Solana leaned against a support beam and slid down it.

"Weird," she said. But her voice didn't sound sassy or condemning. She sounded like she was in wonder.

"Isn't it making idols if we try to draw God?" Becca asked. Then she sighed. "But that's completely innocent and beautiful."

Jacie smiled. "I wonder if Ethel's parents thought the same thing. A kid's idea of God." *So precious and pure.* A door opened inside. Light came into Jacie's own attic.

"There's more," Hannah said, lifting out sheet after sheet of drawings, all by Ethel at ages three and four. People—all heads and stick legs coming out of their heads. Spaghetti fingers and spider-leg lashes around egg-shaped eyes. And more pictures of God. All very similar. A wildness combined with soft curves.

"Do you think I could keep this?" Jacie asked. She wanted to put it on the corkboard in her artist shack. Or maybe in her room. It made her think of God as bigger. Not that she remotely thought this *was* what God looked like. But it threw out of her head the idea that God was a rigid being that someone *could* make a painting or sculpture of. This made it seem more like—

"God is spirit," Hannah quoted from Scripture as she looked at another one. "We can't draw spirits. We can't touch a spirit. Maybe that's what's grabbing at all of us from this thing. It's taking away our solid views of God and letting Him be more, well, unknowable."

Solana nodded. "At the risk of sounding like you guys, I like it because it does exactly that. It makes God seem larger to me. Not shrunk by anyone's particular lack of imagination."

Tyler stepped over piles to give Solana a hug. He kissed her soundly on the cheek. "Sometimes I think you know more than most church people," he said. "You don't put God into a box."

Jacie felt an unseen hand slug her in the stomach. She looked over at Hannah, who looked at her.

Is that what I'm doing, God? I'm putting You into a box of how I want You to be? She closed her eyes a moment. That's exactly what she was doing.

She continued to empty the box in front of her. She dumped more school papers, broken pencils, and crayons into the trash. Reaching below more papers, her hand touched something different. She lifted it out and smiled at it. An old Mickey Mouse pin grinned back at her. *Nora would like this*, she thought. She slipped it into her pocket. She'd give it to her.

Nora has you in a box.

Jacie swallowed hard at that truth. Nora didn't know her at all. She only knew Jacie as a result of one incident and judged her completely for it. Nora formed all her opinions about who Jacie was in every aspect of life because Jacie had accidentally run over her toy.

Jacie squirmed. She didn't want to go where these thoughts led her. She didn't like thinking of herself as being on the same immature level as Nora. After all, things weren't the same. At least Jacie hadn't known about the toy lurking behind her tire. God, on the other hand, *could have* stopped the train accident. Even if most accidents and illnesses are just a part of life, God could have done something to prevent Dinah from getting into the doomed car at that moment. She could have been blocked by kids playing in the aisle. Greg could have been talking to her, teasing her like he always did.

But no. God let it happen.

She fought the tears and looked with shame into the box. She was judging all God's character by this one incident, condemning Him without considering there may be more. She was trying to squeeze God tightly into her tiny uninformed, limiting box. She had thrown out everything she knew about Him because one person died young.

Two people, she reminded herself. Dinah *and* the baby.

chapter 14

"Here," Jacie said, holding out her hand to Nora.

"What?" Nora crabbed. She glared at Jacie like public enemy number one.

"Here," Jacie said again.

Nora finally shifted her gaze to see what Jacie had in her palm. Her eyes lit up.

"Do you want him?"

Nora nodded, her eyes not leaving the colorful pin.

"Can I put him on you?"

Nora looked at Jacie with suspicion.

"It's okay. I'll make sure he stays on good and tight."

"Okay," Nora relented, still eyeing Jacie cautiously.

Jacie hoped that she wouldn't accidentally stab Nora. That would be the end for good. Nora stood very still while Jacie put her finger behind the pin to guide it through Nora's shirt. "There!"

Nora looked proud. She looked down at her chest with Mickey hanging there. She looked up at Jacie and slipped her hand inside Jacie's.

"Shall we go show your mom?" Jacie asked, hoping that she'd not look like such a bad guy. She wondered if Camerin was beginning to believe that Jacie was the ogre Nora thought.

Nora took off at a dead run. Or tried to. With Jacie in tow, Nora only succeeded in trying to yank Jacie's arm from its socket. Jacie laughed and started to trot, making sure she kept behind her just enough to let Nora be in control.

• • •

Over the next week, all the *Brios* talked about the attic. The Historical Society was delighted at how much they'd completed. They agreed to let them go through the journals, giving them literature on how to read for historical significance.

Jacie thought a lot about Nora and the little girl's changing attitude toward her. She liked that Nora skipped and jumped when Jacie came home. She wore her pin every day. She stopped putting toy land mines in the parking area behind cars.

"Mom says I can go with you to art class," she said. "Can I still? Can I?"

"Of course you can come," Jacie said, figuring nothing worse could happen in her art class than what was already happening week after week. She didn't even know why the people kept coming back when all they did was grumble through the entire thing.

Wednesday, Hannah showed up at school, looking almost as bad as she had the first week after Aunt Dinah's death.

"Can I call a meeting in Alyeria?" she asked, her voice tremulous.

"No," Solana said matter-of-factly. "Just because we invited you a couple of times—"

"Sol!" Becca said, moving to hug Hannah. "What's wrong with you?"

"Why?" Jacie asked, noticing Hannah's trembling lip.

She held out an envelope. By the looks of it, it had either had a bad trip through the postal system, or it had been read many times. Jacie was drawn to the deep purples and ivory designs. It looked like something out of an Impressionist painting. "It's a letter from Aunt Dinah."

No one spoke. Everyone looked at the letter as if it had been directly delivered from heaven. Or as if she'd written it right before the accident. Hannah had already gotten one eerie letter like that delivered a week after her death.

"Hannah," Solana said quietly. "*Amiga*. Your Aunt Dinah has been dead for a few months. Where has the letter been?"

"Because of working in the attic, I thought, well, I thought about cleaning my own closet." She sighed a wobbly breath as if tears were about to come. "She wrote me lots of letters and postcards from around the world. I have a boxful. I finally decided to read them all again. To feel closer to her, you know?"

Jacie understood. She did all kinds of things over the years to feel closer to her dad.

"She wrote this one a little over three years ago."

Jacie hoped Hannah didn't notice the collective sigh.

"She liked writing me letters at milestones, and since I was in the first semester of high school . . ."

"At home," Solana said, clarifying.

"Yeah . . . she always gave me words to live by or something. Anyway, this one . . ." Hannah took in a quick breath and let out a sob. "I'm sorry," she whispered. She turned and walked away, sobs shaking her shoulders.

That afternoon, the group gathered in uncomfortable silence—which Solana immediately broke. "We don't come here for fun anymore," she complained, dropping to the log in Alyeria.

Hannah looked as though someone had slapped her. "I'm sorry. We can—"

Solana rolled her eyes. "Hannah. I'm just talking. I wanna hear your letter."

Tyler settled in next to Jacie, a bit closer than usual, she thought. It was as if on its own, her body leaned into him.

Hannah took the letter from her bag like a fragile object. The envelope bore the clean slice of an opener across the top. She removed the sheets, unfolded them, and swallowed hard. She sighed deeply and wiped at a tear. "I can do this," she whispered to herself. She cleared her throat and sat up straighter.

Dearest Hannah-girl,

I don't know why, but I want to kind of journal stuff to you. I've been thinking a lot, and figured you were the one who would listen.

Right after my "bad girl days" in high school, I finally gave my whole life over to God for however long He chooses it to be. I wanted my entire life from there on out to be a joyous service—even if it's only being kind to the grumpy store clerk. I suppose this is, in part, because none of us knows how long our lives will last, and so we can't, or shouldn't, live timidly for God. Otherwise, we've wasted those short days. (And from what I've heard, even old folks say the days of life are short.)

Once I made that decision, I didn't fear dying anymore because I knew that by living for God every moment—even in the small moments (like when I'm cleaning my apartment—ugh!—or cooking mac 'n' cheese for dinner)—that there would be no regrets. No wasted time. You can't fear death when you are too busy to think about it! You also don't fear death if you trust God with every moment of life.

Hannah, none of us knows whether we will live to be 93 like Great Gran, or 32, like her brother Brad who we never even met. The point is, we have to trust God with our whole life. Whether that's 10 years or 10 hundred years.

If there's nothing else I teach you as your crazy Aunt Dinah, this would be it—live life abundantly. Full and adventurous, serving God with all your heart, and personality, and gifts, making the bigger, riskier choice, not the smaller, safer one. Make the odd choice, rather than the normal, expected one. I hope when I face Him on that day, it can be with a satisfaction that nothing was left undone, done half-heartedly, or missed because I wanted to be safe and ordinary. God loves adventure!

In a few short years you'll be out of high school and off to college, then into the world. No matter what life throws at you, good or bad, Hannah, go for it! (And you will have plenty of really bad stuff in your life. Count on it.) Live great and big and full, knowing God never, ever promised us happiness. He only promised He'd be there, using every life event to mold us, teach us, and train us.

Your wacky Aunt Dinah won't always be around to kick you in the behind and get you out of your room and out into the world, but God will always, always be there.

With hugs until the end of time,

Aunt Dinah

Hannah wiped her eyes. "Do you think Aunt Dinah knew she'd die?" she asked, folding the Impressionist stationery in her lap.

No one spoke for a moment. The aspens quaked their leaves with a soft, tumbly, comforting sound.

"No," Becca said, finally. "But I do think she knew that life is hard. That we make huge mistakes—" Becca stopped, obviously remembering her role in the disastrous fire at the Community Center. Her lip trembled.

"Or that life isn't the happy fairy tale we imagined," Jacie added. "There are no happy endings. No matter what we do—right or wrong—it can dump good things or bad things on us."

Becca let a few tears gently roll down her cheeks, unchecked. "We can't let the bad things destroy us. We have to let God use them to teach us."

Tyler jumped up. "You guys are missing her point entirely," he said. "Yeah, life isn't perfect and God will use all that. But she's saying to live every moment as though it were your last. Take the risky step. Go live in Italy, Jacie, and learn to paint. Take a European semester. Trust that God will provide the money. Becca, you see what needs to be done to help others, and you dive in to do something about it." He paced back and forth, his finger jabbing the air for emphasis. "Living for God doesn't mean pining away, or dreading the future, or being careful about every little thing."

Jacie's head snapped up, looking him in the eyes. "It's jumping in, moving forward when you can only see one step at a time."

"YES!" Tyler said, grabbing her shoulders and pulling her up. "Even when that step is hard." He spun her around. "It's dancing through the darkness."

Jacie giggled as the aspens blurred in her vision.

"It's designing a program for kids to go on a ropes course and listening to them whoop and holler," Becca said.

Solana beamed. "It's finding dragonflies and boreal toads and helping to preserve them."

Hannah kept staring at her aunt's letter. Whether she was listening or not, Jacie couldn't tell.

A startling thought flashed like a photo in Jacie's mind. She flopped back down. "But look at Christians in other countries.

They have it horrible. They are living the New Testament nightmare of being tortured and killed. Persecuted. How can we expect any less? How can we even think that being a Christian means a happy life?"

Hannah looked up, her eyes wide and sad, yet without tears. "We can't. I always thought that being the right girl would make my life easy. That by following God's list of rules, I would be doing the right thing, and so my life would be the perfect American dream. But God isn't American, is He?"

They all looked at her.

They looked at each other.

Jacie closed her eyes and thought about it.

Solana sucked in a whole lot of air. "Wow."

Jacie opened her eyes. Solana paced back and forth, shaking her head. "Wow," she said again. "You've probably said the most profound thing I've ever heard," Solana said. She continued to shake her head, as if trying to line up the thoughts.

"Share," Tyler demanded.

"I think that's what's been bugging me for so long," she said. "That all the Christians here seem to think that America is the center of God's universe."

Becca untied her shoes, tightened the laces, and retied them.

"We live as if that's true, don't we?" Tyler said, his frenetic pacing halted.

"As if God wants us to be happy," Becca said.

Jacie tipped her head back and watched the light play off the silver undersides of the aspen leaves. "This is why I can't trust Him," she said. "This is why I can't trust Him with my future. God doesn't stop the persecution of Christians around the world. God doesn't put our happiness first. He cares most that we obey Him. He cares more for His kingdom than anything else."

"What's your option then?" Solana asked, shocking them all with her sudden ability to speak seriously about God. "If you don't trust God, then what?"

Jacie considered. Ultimately, in the very frightening, very unknown of eternity, God did promise happiness. But here on earth? Here was unknown, too. Unknown if God would allow an early, awful death. Or heartaches. Or poverty. He wasn't so concerned about happy things as with depth of character. He wasn't so concerned about life on this earth as benefits for eternity. If Jacie's death was going to do something better for eternity, He'd take her life.

And that's what scared her.

"Are you there?" Solana asked, her face large and close to Jacie's.

"I'm sorry," Jacie said, still seeing herself shivering with fear in a corner of God's enormous world. "What were you saying?"

"We were agreeing with you that God doesn't care about our individual happiness, but wanting desperately to disagree," Becca said.

"As God," Hannah was saying as she stared at the letter in her lap, "can't He care about the corporate good of His kingdom *and* the individual at the same time?" She sounded as if she hoped she could convince herself.

Jacie stared at Hannah and felt the rain of her words shower upon her. Something shifted inside her. She knew something so clearly that it shocked her with its truth and terror. She would have to throw herself into the painting, not knowing how it would end up. Whether the painter would choose dark colors or bright. Whether the painting would be dark, fierce, and true, or bright, happy, and full of sunshine. She was powerless to make it come out one way or the other. But if she did cooperate, it had the potential to be all those things, one that would bring many to respect the painter.

She shivered with the thought.

Could she do it? Did she believe it? She felt as though she stood at the edge of a huge canyon. The chasm before her loomed like an open mouth to devour her.

And she couldn't jump.

She just couldn't.

chapter 15

"I think Aunt Dinah wants me to live," Hannah said.

"Um. Yeah," Solana said.

"No. I mean, I think she wants me to dive in . . ." Tears poured down Hannah's face. She wiped them away with the back of her hand, creating dust streaks across her cheeks. "And trust God . . ."

"And?" Becca asked, leaning forward.

"I want you guys to help me."

Everyone nodded except Jacie. She couldn't help someone else yet.

Tyler squatted in front of Hannah. He took both her hands in his. "Do you think she'd want you to go to the prom?"

She grinned. "Only with you, Tyler Jennings."

"Not with Grant?" he asked.

She smiled. "Aunt Dinah supported my vow of courtship 100 percent. So she'd know I would choose not to go on even one date with him." She smiled. "Besides, how could I not go with you guys? We're going to have so much fun."

Tyler stood, puffing out his chest. "Yep. That would be the full truth."

"How can we help?" Becca asked.

Hannah shrugged. "I know I'm swinging back and forth between accepting Dinah's death and being furious and untrusting. So I guess you can help by reminding me sometimes of Dinah's letter. You can ask me if I'm really living."

Solana clapped her hands together and rubbed them with glee. "Oooo yeah, baby! I get to get on Hannah's case. I've been waiting a long time for this."

Hannah looked up at her and grinned. "Now that you have permission, will things really be any different?"

Pantomiming touching his finger to something hot, Tyler said, "Ssssst!"

Jacie watched it all, wishing their words could penetrate this great wall she'd built around herself. She wanted to give in. She didn't want to give in.

She just didn't want to be scared anymore.

• • •

"I'm ready," Nora screamed through Jacie's front door as she pounded on it with her little fist. For such a small thing she could really pack a wallop.

Jacie opened the door to an apron-frocked Nora who shrieked when Grace swamped her face with lavish lickings.

Once Jacie pulled Grace away and made her sit on her little rug, she could see Nora had a pink blanket edged with worn pink satin pinned around her neck. She wore a tiara on her head. She gripped a giant foot-long pencil in one hand and a tablet of paper in the other.

"Mom says I have to wear a seatbelt and sit in the backseat. Can Grace come?"

"No, Grace can't come. You're a little early. Let me get my stuff."

She gathered her bags and purse and off they went.

Nora jabbered the entire time. "Where's your art class? How long does it take to get there? Are we there yet? Why can't Grace come? Do you have snacks? Can I have snack? I'm thirsty. Can I have a drink? I have to go potty. Are we there yet? Are we going to paint? I love to paint, that's why Mommy said I have to wear my apron. Are we going to draw? I like to draw. I draw pictures and Mommy puts them on the refrigerator. Does your Mommy put your pictures on the refrigerator? Are we there yet?"

Without Nora stopping for answers, Jacie could just drive and listen, nodding where it seemed appropriate. She wondered about Camerin's sanity. Having a nonstop talker would make her crazy. At the moment, she wondered how she'd make it through class. Between Nora, Marlene, and grumpy Brenda, she wondered about the survival techniques of teachers and how she might learn them in five minutes or less.

Once at the shelter, Nora continued to talk. She talked while Jacie gave her little jobs to do. She talked when people came in. But when the door opened and Marlene's grandmother wheeled her up to the table, Nora shut up. She stared at Marlene, her mouth slack, her eyes wide. She dropped her things onto the table and walked up to her. "What's her name?"

"Marlene," said the grandmother.

"Does she get to stay?"

Grandmother nodded. To Jacie she said, "She's doin' better, ain't she?"

Jacie smiled. "Yes, she is." But Jacie didn't really know. *Same as always.*

Grandmother left, and Jacie faced her class. "We have a new girl today," she said, groaning inside at how she sounded like all the grade-school teachers she'd known. "This is Nora."

But Nora didn't face the class. She didn't even acknowledge the class. She hung over Marlene's tray, talking softly to her.

Jacie opened her bags and brought out lots of homemade Play-Doh in different colors. Her mom had helped her come up with that idea. Maybe they need something to sink their hands into. She passed out tubs of it and asked Gina to show the other little kids how to roll the dough in their hands to make balls. She put out things she had made—fortunately she wasn't as good with sculpting, so her pieces did not look so finished. She hoped that would help them at least try.

She moved closer to Nora and Marlene, hoping Nora wouldn't notice.

". . . and she has a doggie named Grace. Do you have a dog?"

Marlene's head nodded like a horse.

"Do you play with your doggie?"

Marlene groaned up and down the scale.

"I wish I had a doggie that liked to play with me."

The exchange went on. Nora asking, Marlene grunting and making sounds that could be words.

Jacie knelt beside Nora. "Marlene. Do you want to try some clay?"

Marlene nodded.

"What color?"

Marlene's groans stuttered. Jacie looked at Nora.

"Blue is her favorite color," Nora said, still looking at Marlene adoringly.

Jacie got some blue clay and gave it to Nora. Nora looked at her, then set the clay in front of Marlene. She looked back at Marlene. "Whatcha gonna make?"

Marlene groaned and whacked at the clay. But instead of pounding it, her hand hit it and knocked it across the room.

"Good job!" Nora said, giggling. Marlene guffawed.

"Jacie," Roberta called.

Jacie turned to go help the little girl, while secretly watching Nora and Marlene in amazement.

By the end of the hour, almost everyone had created something they were proud of. After Jacie had showed them how to make baskets and bird nests with eggs, almost everyone had made one. Ricky surprised them all by making a fabulous alien-warrior.

"Wow," Gina said. "That's really good."

Ricky looked like he was about to smash it because no self-respecting boy could have a compliment like that from a girl.

"Dude," Eric said, "that's the coolest thing."

Ricky smiled.

The biggest surprise came from Marlene's tray. Nora had helped her flatten a large piece of clay, then gave her things to swipe through it, creating interesting lines and squiggles.

Nora looked up at Jacie and said reverently, "She says it's God."

Jacie looked at the beautiful, lively design on the clay and swallowed hard. She thought of three-year-old Ethel's drawing on the corkboard wall in her studio.

She sat on a chair so she could look into Marlene's eyes. She didn't feel Marlene was really "there" but maybe she was. Maybe there was something bigger and deeper than Jacie would ever realize. "This is God?" she asked.

Marlene nodded. Her guttural noises came as heavy words. She could pick up one here and there, but Nora translated like a second language. "Strong. Powerful. Pretty. Love. Good. Holds me. Sings to me," Nora said.

And then Marlene spoke, her eyes suddenly full of life and

boring into Jacie's. She lifted her arm, her pointed finger waving in Jacie's general direction. "Gawwwd auvvs hew."

"God loves you," Nora said.

Jacie bit her lip and nodded, tears welling up in her eyes. *Words from heaven.*

Somebody thumped her on the back. "Best class ever, Teach," Ricky said.

Brenda nodded, holding up a basket full of eggs, but not looking in Marlene's direction. "Yeah. Look what I done."

Jacie wanted to say something, but her heart was too full.

● ● ●

"Somebody zip me up," Solana demanded. "I'll ruin my nails."

"Hold on," Hannah said, poking another bobby pin into her hair. She'd braided and twisted alternate strands across the top and sides of her head, then pulled the rest of her long locks into a messy bun. The result was stunning.

"Me, too," Becca said, turning her back to Hannah.

Hannah zipped.

Jacie kept taking deep breaths. *Prom.* The only one she'd ever have. She kept wanting to cry. It was either PMS or the realization that this was the countdown.

"Does *Prom* come from *Promise*?" Hannah asked. "I mean is this where guys used to promise their lives to their girlfriends?"

"Wow," Sol said. "Never thought of that. Maybe." She twisted to try to see the backside of herself in the mirror. "Can you see my dragonfly okay?"

Becca patted Solana's shoulder. "It looks fabulous."

"How about my tattoo?" Hannah asked, tilting her head so Jacie's temporary artwork of a gentle butterfly showed a little better.

"Perfect," Sol said. "I think you should get a real one."

Hannah blew a raspberry. "No thanks. I like something I can take off at the end of the evening."

"You sure you don't want one?" Jacie asked Becca.

Becca forced a smile. Everyone knew she was barely holding it together. All she could think about was that Nate was far away in Australia. They knew she didn't intend to have a good time but would do her best for the rest of them. "No thanks."

Jacie looked at her hair from one side to the other. She wanted some springy curls to hang down. But not too many. And not in a uniform shape around her head. She didn't want to look like somebody's bad idea of curtains.

"Can we pray?" Hannah blurted. "I'm so nervous I can't stand it. I know this isn't a real date. But, shoot. I'm still trembling as if it were."

Jacie pulled the satin cords on Hannah's corset, tying them and making sure the loops matched exactly. "Do you think God might be mad at you?"

Hannah looked over her shoulder at Jacie. She smiled big. "No. I'm living life. I'm staying true to my beliefs, but I'm still living as big as I can."

Jacie hugged her and blinked back her tears. The transformation in Hannah since she dug up that old letter grew every day. She still had her doubts, but she went to God with everything now—as if her relationship with Him didn't hinge upon rules, or doubts, or pat answers, or things going well, or people living or dying. Jacie wanted the faith that Hannah was growing. But she didn't know how.

"I need to use the restroom," Solana said. "You guys go ahead without me."

"Please stay," Hannah said. "I won't make you pray. Just be here so we're complete."

Solana made a face, crossed her arms, and leaned against the door.

"God," Hannah began after holding hands with the girls on either side of her. "I'm nervous. Scared. I've never been to a dance before. But I want to have fun with my friends, if that's okay with You. I can't thank You enough for bringing these wonderful girls into my life. I hope that You'll like the dance since You'll be there with us. Oh. And help Tyler to have fun with us, too. Amen."

A knock came at the door, and Solana opened it. Jacie's mom stood there, dressed in nice clothes. "Tyler's here," she whispered.

"You going out, Mom?" Jacie asked.

Her mom nodded. Jacie hated that her mom went out almost every weekend now. And she talked an awful lot on the phone in the bedroom. She and Grace went on many hikes with Rich and his dog, Sydney.

Becca walked by and said, "Have a great time!"

"Don't stay out too late," Solana said as she swished by in red satin.

Hannah pecked Jacie's mom on the cheek. "I'm so happy for you," she said. She reached behind herself and grabbed Jacie's hand and gave it a quick squeeze. "Let's go. We have our own date."

Jacie heard the meaning behind Hannah's words. *Let your mom live!*

Jacie stopped and kissed her mom on the cheek. "Say hi to Rich for me." She gulped, and fought the battle of emotions tearing around inside her.

"I put Grace in my bedroom," her mom said after them. "I didn't want dog hair—"

Tyler stood at the dining room table, dressed in a traditional tux, an array of plastic flower boxes around him.

Jacie couldn't believe how incredible he looked. Suddenly grown up. Not a boy, but a man.

"Let's go down one at a time," Solana said. She shoved Becca. "You first."

Becca stepped down the stairs moving more like a princess than an athlete.

Tyler picked up a box and presented it to Becca. She lifted out a white orchid. "It's gorgeous."

He fumbled around a bit, but managed to pin it onto Becca's royal blue dress. He gave her a quick, light kiss on her cheek. "From Nate," he said.

Hannah went next. He presented her with an ivory rose to go with her peach corset gown. They both flushed when he pecked her cheek.

Solana waltzed down the stairs, her nose so far in the air, Jacie was surprised she didn't trip.

"Princess Solana," Tyler said with a sweeping bow. He took a white rose and went to pin it onto her. He looked at her, confused. He looked at the other girls.

"Pin it," Solana ordered.

"Where?" Tyler whispered, his face flushing.

"Oh, I'll do it." Solana grabbed the flower from him and stabbed it onto her strapless dress.

Jacie was still laughing when Tyler motioned for her to come down.

She felt silly. But then she looked at Tyler's face. He took in her eyes, her hair, her face. She thought she'd melt before she could reach the bottom of the stairs. There he presented her with a rich purplish-gray rose.

"A sterling silver rose . . ." He stopped mid-sentence. He took a breath and a step toward her. He pinned it onto her dress, then whispered in her ear, ". . . for my sterling silver girl." He kissed her on the cheek, but it was more than a peck. It lingered just a moment. Jacie's heart leapt and began to run at full gallop. He stepped back.

There. In his eyes again.

FLASH!

"Mom!"

"I need lots of pictures of these memorable moments. Okay everyone, sit on the sofa." Small, plaintive yips came from upstairs. "Grace! Hush! Momma's taking pictures of Jacie."

Jacie tried to hold back a giggle. She failed miserably and within a second the others joined in.

Jacie's mom gave them all a look. "Okay. Fine. So I'm a weird dog person."

"We can't sit," Hannah said. "Our dresses will get wrinkled."

"You'll be sitting in the car in three minutes," Tyler said.

"I want everyone to see my entire dress," Solana said.

Jacie's mom took pictures of everyone in every conceivable mix until finally Jacie said, "Mom. The prom isn't that long. We'd really like to experience some of it."

"How are we all going to fit into Tyler's car?" Hannah asked.

Tyler grinned. He threw open the front door and waved his hand as if showing the prize they'd won. In the parking lot, with Nora dancing around and talking nonstop, was a gentleman dressed in a tux and gloves and top hat, standing next to a silver Rolls-Royce limousine.

Tyler insisted on escorting the girls two at a time down the stairs with their hands nestled in his crooked arm. The limo driver opened the rear doors and helped the ladies inside.

Jacie felt dreamy and off balance. She closed her eyes to soak in the perfume, the scent of flowers, Tyler's aftershave, and to replay his expression as he watched her come down the stairs.

"Whose house first?" he asked.

"My parents need to put the kids to bed soon," Hannah said.

“To Hannah’s,” Tyler said to the driver.

He tipped his hat. “Yes, sir.”

The driver then picked up a phone and dialed something. “We’re on our way,” he said crisply.

Hannah’s mom called the rest of the parents, and all gathered at the Connors’ home so the *Brios* wouldn’t have to drive all over town. A half an hour later, their faces cramped with frozen smiles, they were free—free to make a long-standing dream come true.

chapter 16

Jacie absorbed the evening as though living in a movie of her own. The dark room filled with beautiful girls in beautiful clothes. Boys she'd known for years acted more like men in their tuxes. She'd dreamed of this ever since she learned about proms in elementary school. She wanted the dream to be true.

A mirrored disco ball scattered colored lights, spattering the floor with diamonds of blue, red, green, yellow, purple, and white. Couples moved to the music, some of them in rather raunchy ways, others as far apart as you could get and still touch. In the dark corners, couples nuzzled and kissed.

Solana sat, her arms crossed on the table, leaning to talk to the guy sitting on the other side. Jacie didn't think Solana knew how NOT to flirt, even though she didn't mean to. The guy's date, Amanda, looked ticked.

"Where are you going to school in the fall, Ryan?" Solana asked.

"Copper Ridge Community."

"Really? That's where our date, Tyler, might be going."

Ryan leaned forward, cutting Amanda completely out of the conversation. "So how'd this dude-friend of yours manage to get *four* beautiful women to go to the prom with him?" He looked around, a sly grin on his face. "You guys always do things *together*?"

His disgusting attitude was more than Jacie could stand. "I'm going to the ladies' room," she said, shoving her chair back and jumping up. "Go with me, Sol?"

"Stay," Ryan said.

"Go," mouthed Amanda, her eyes spitting poison.

Solana looked at Ryan and gave him a cursory smile. "You know us girls. Can't go without a friend."

"He's a jerk," Jacie said as they left.

Solana shrugged. "So what else is new?"

"This is so amazing," Jacie said, absorbing everything.

"I refuse to be sarcastic and snotty," Solana said. "So unlike me. And I won't admit it on Monday. But this is better than I'd thought. I didn't want to come without Ramón, but I hated to let Tyler down, so here I am. And you know what? This is more fun than being alone with a guy."

"You really think?"

Solana smiled, swishing her dress for maximum viewing benefit. "I do. Tyler's a gem. Dinner with all of my best friends without some idiot guy drooling over me. Being able to be myself. It's like Alyeria dressed up and on the town." She looked around as if someone could hear them over the din. "I will remember this night always."

Jacie couldn't believe there were tears in Solana's eyes.

"It's your turn!" Tyler said, appearing from nowhere to interrupt the moment. He held out his hand.

Solana beamed at Jacie and took his hand. The two disappeared into the rhythmic crowd.

"I danced!" Hannah exclaimed, holding both of Jacie's hands, her eyes sparkling. "I'm a total klutz, but I danced. Did you see me?"

"Anyone can be a klutz and dance to that song. It was made for that."

Hannah threw back her head. "I don't care! I danced."

"Will your parents care?" Jacie asked, not wanting Hannah's joy to be spoiled by needing to stand up to her parents.

Hannah shook her head. "Mom had a long talk with me about how it's not dancing they think is bad, but that so many people use it as an excuse to move in seductive ways that are unfair to their dance partner. After her lecture, she taught me how to dance!"

Jacie watched Tyler try to twirl Solana, but she stood her ground.

"Tyler took swing lessons," Hannah said.

"He did?"

"Just for prom. He said he wanted us to have a lot of fun."

Jacie kept her eyes on Tyler and Solana. She danced better than anyone Jacie knew. That girl could move! She made Tyler look ridiculous, but you could tell neither of them cared.

"Where's Becca?"

Jacie pointed at the table of the girl basketball jocks with their boyfriends. "She's been making the rounds."

"I need to get my camera and do the same," Hannah said. "I've got a spread to do for the *Times* next Friday."

"No Galvin limbo pictures I hope."

Hannah softly backhanded her. "Thanks for reminding me."

"No problem." Jacie couldn't resist reminding Hannah of

the homecoming spread she had developed. A jealous girl had wanted to ruin Hannah's reputation by inserting a photo that made it seem she was about to kiss the new boy.

"See you around," Hannah said. "Keep looking gorgeous. I want to get a good picture of the *Brios* for the spread."

Jacie stood at the edge of the dance floor, moving to the beat. Little thoughts kept nibbling at her, trying to get her attention.

No, she told herself. *I'm here to have fun*, she reminded herself.

But as much as she tried, it all felt lacking somehow, like she betrayed her best friend to go with someone else.

What was that about? Where'd it come from?

Tyler trotted up to her, Solana tagging along behind, attached to his hand. He kissed his fingers and put them against Solana's cheek. "Thank you. Fabulous dance."

"Likewise," Solana said. "Now I'm going to find someone to steal for another dance." She got an evil grin. "I know! Dennis!"

"He's here?" Jacie asked, scanning the crowd for the geeky boy who used to follow Solana like a puppy dog.

"Yeah. I want to give him one last thrill before graduation."

"SOL!" Jacie said.

"She'll never change, Jacie," Tyler said. He still threw Solana an affectionate smile. But she'd waved and was gone, weaving through the crowd.

Tyler turned and bowed to Jacie. "May I have this dance?"

Jacie curtsied. "Why, of course."

She hesitated when she realized it was a slow song. Tyler continued to hold out his hand. She looked beyond him to couples who rubbed their bodies so close, she thought they should be dancing in private.

"Close your eyes," Tyler told her.

She nodded. It was so like him to know what she was thinking. And how often had she known what *he* was thinking?

When he took her in his arms, she tried not to feel the warmth and safety that flooded through. She put her arms around his neck. He put his around her waist. Their cheeks so close together. She smelled Polo Sport. Closing her eyes heightened things. Snapshot memories played in a series in her mind. Him tossing her into Becca's pool a thousand times. Hours of talking. On the telephone. Over coffee. In Alyeria. In Venezuela trying to save her from Gregg. Taking care of her when she was sick. In his costume when they were little kids playing Narnia in Alyeria. Popping into her artist's shack windblown and adorable.

No.

Had she ever been as connected to anyone as she was to Tyler? How many times had he called her with girl problems and her heart ached?

No.

She opened her eyes. Tufts of Tyler's hair so close. His soft, gum-minted breath on her ear. She swallowed and fought back emotions.

The song ended too soon.

Had they played a shortened version? She felt gypped. She wanted more.

Tyler held on a moment longer. Then said, "Dipping you!" and he dipped her! He pulled her up, his eyes not leaving hers.

"Why did you do that?" she asked. She didn't know whether to laugh or be mortified.

"For fun. I want everyone to see Tyler Jennings dancing with the prettiest girl in the school."

"Tyler!" a voice called. "Tyler. Can you and I dance?"

Jessica Abbot. Jacie felt a rise of protection tightening her jaw. "Do you want to dance with her?" she hissed.

Tyler shrugged. "Sure. I guess."

Jessica gave Jacie one of her sweetest fake smiles. "Thanks, Jace. You're always so sweet." The tiny girl with the perfect figure and most expensive dress in the room swept Tyler onto the floor. Jacie glared after her, glad the deejay had put on another fast song. She didn't think Jessica could move very well in that tight dress. She hoped she'd split a seam.

"Want to dance?" a voice asked from behind.

She turned to smile at Damien. "What about Robin?"

"I asked her if it was all right for one dance. She likes you. It's okay."

Jacie let him lead her out to the floor. She let her mind go and her body move to the music. She opened herself up to it. The more she allowed it in, the easier it was. She smiled at Damien, and suddenly pictures from their past flashed in her head. A hike. Smashed sandwiches. Forbidden kisses, stolen in moments of time. Showing him around the first day. His eyes.

She shook her head a little to clear the thoughts away. She let the music take over. It was odd. The memories grabbed her, but they didn't hold her heart the way they used to. Not like memories of Tyler. Instead, the pictures pointed her to the end of their relationship. They led her to things she didn't want to think about. The painting. The hurt it represented. The horrible story of the boy he accidentally hit with the car. The boy's death a few days later.

Jacie felt the music slipping away, her movements awkward as if she tried to bat away the sadness.

Damien smiled. He held her shoulders and slowed their dancing to say in her ear, "I'm so glad to have known you, Jacie."

Jacie blushed. "Those were my bad girl days. I wanted you more than I wanted what was right," she called into his ear.

"You weren't such a bad girl. You were my turning point, you know."

"Me?" She cocked her head and pointed at herself. She felt tears gathering in a storm behind her eyes. In her chest. Their dancing had forgotten to pay attention to the beat.

He nodded. He took her shoulders again, stopping their dance completely. "It was your painting. It opened the door. God had forgiven me. I could forgive myself. It still haunts me." He put her at arm's length and looked her directly in the eyes. His sincerity almost unleashed the storm.

She wanted to talk. But the dance floor at prom was no place for it. Besides, his words did things inside her she didn't want anymore. They unlocked everything—her questions about Dinah, about who God really is, the hurt she'd have to face and the uncertainty about life if she let the questions out.

The song ended. Damien took her hand and led her off the floor. "Keep in touch, okay?"

Jacie nodded. She loved Damien. Not the way Solana loved Ramón.

Not the way you love Tyler.

She stomped that thought out of existence.

I'm thinking about Damien. I care a lot about him.

Beautiful girls in beautiful dresses swished by her. The music slammed into her, loud and pushy. Sweaty guys stripped their outer jackets and loosened bow ties.

She thought about what she'd told him—that those were her bad girl days. Why had she said that? The words from Aunt Dinah's letter had haunted her. Were these her bad girl days? Were all her days bad girl days? Pushing God away so she didn't have to deal with Him certainly didn't make her a good girl. The old Hannah would be scolding her up one side and down the other. The new Hannah reassured her she could kick and scream all she wanted, but God still wanted her. After all, if He could forgive Hannah's actions since Dinah's death and love her anyway, He could still love Jacie as well.

The rest of the evening Jacie tried to look at the event the way Solana did: the last big party for the Alyeria gang, to love and enjoy each of her friends as though today were their last day. She laughed. She took turns dancing with Tyler. They all danced with Tyler at the same time. She danced with Becca and Sol. She spun, she twirled. But her heart seemed roped to the questions.

chapter 17

Jacie didn't sleep much at all that night. The next morning, she woke early and left her mom a note. There was only one place she knew to go.

Jacie went to Alyeria.

When she got there, she stood, looking up through the budding aspen trees to the rich blue sky above. She turned, slowly, pivoting on her clunky shoe, hoping God would see her, would call to her in a way she could hear, or show Himself through the branches of the trees. "I'm desperate, God," she whispered. "I want You. I need You. I don't trust You. I want You to go away."

Jacie listened. Nothing. Birds scurrying around in the brush. Blackbirds scolding something. But no voice. No reassuring thoughts. Nothing. God had to speak to her about Aunt Dinah. He owed her that much, didn't He? To explain what He'd done and why.

She dropped to her knees, touching her forehead to the dirt

like a Muslim man in prayer. At least a Muslim knew which direction to turn in prayer. She didn't know where to turn, or how to reach out, how to connect with God.

She knelt there, hunched over, thoughts painfully silent. But she couldn't even drag up the anger or the frustration of recent days. Clawing at her mind, she tried to open the wounds and fury and questions she had for God. Yet none came.

Certainly she did not have peace. Silence did not automatically guarantee peace. Silence was only lack of sound.

Jacie took deep breaths. Or, rather, they took her. They grabbed her lungs and filled them with air, then forced them out. Fast. Hard. She sniffled and dust went up her nose. She wiped at it, but wanted to stay in this position of humility before God. Surely He'd come speak to her if she stayed hunched over this way. Surely He'd see how important it was for her to understand. How their very relationship depended on it. If she could not understand God's choices, how could she trust Him with her future? How could she agree to follow a God who might snuff her out in the next instant? Or the next year? Or 10 years from now? How could she possibly live without fear every day of her life, never knowing if each moment was to be her last?

She closed her eyes. She waited. She waited. She waited.

Her neck grew stiff. Her fingertips became numb.

She waited.

God didn't say a word.

She squeezed her eyes shut harder. She tried to block out all her daydreams about prom. She kept picturing Tyler taking her hand and leading her to the dance floor. But she shouldn't be thinking that. She shouldn't be thinking about how he'd looked at her. Or his kiss on her cheek. Nor how nice he smelled.

She shook her head, the dirt getting in her hair. *Listen, Jacie. Listen for God.*

But she couldn't keep thoughts out of her head long enough to hear God's voice.

She took another deep breath and focused on what she had come for.

"I knew I'd find you here."

Jacie bolted upright, her heart pounding as if God had come and sat right in front of her. But it wasn't God. It was only Tyler. Then Solana. Then Becca.

Becca sat in front of Jacie and dusted her hair. "You can't do this anymore, Jace. You've got to come out of it."

Solana looked troubled. "I know it's hard. But you can't stay like this."

"What do you expect me to do?" Jacie snapped. "I want this to be over too."

"Then walk away," Solana said.

"Let God be God," Becca said. "Give it to Him."

Jacie gritted her teeth. "Look. I'd give it to Him if I could. But I don't trust Him."

"You can't just give up your faith."

Solana said nothing.

"I don't intend to," Jacie said. "But I've got to make sense of this, or I'll go crazy. Things don't match up. If God said He loved Dinah, then why in the world did He have her step into that train car? He could have done anything, but He didn't. Is that love? Is that love for the unborn baby?"

"Babies die," Solana said softly.

"And have you forgiven God for taking your baby brother?" Jacie asked.

Solana sighed.

Tyler leaned against a tree and said nothing. Jacie looked at him. Their eyes locked for a moment, but Jacie could not read his. Hers, she knew, flashed with the anger she felt.

"Where's Hannah?" Jacie asked.

Solana jerked her head toward the opening in the trees. "Out in the car."

Jacie stormed out of the clearing. She yanked the door open and stared at Hannah, who sat with her head bowed. Praying? Jacie crumbled, sliding into the backseat and taking Hannah's hand. Hannah looked up and bit her lip, watching Jacie through round, sad eyes. Without a word, they connected. Two girls whose faith shattered in one moment of time. Two girls who had relied on that faith to see them through every aspect of life.

After a few moments, Jacie whispered, "I can't do it."

Hannah nodded, tears welling up. She said nothing.

Tyler's face appeared through the window as he bent over to look inside the car. "That's it," he said. He went around to the other side and offered his hand to Jacie.

She looked at it, and looked at him.

"I want to show you something," he said softly. "Come with me."

Jacie sighed and let him lead her out of the car toward his.

● ● ●

"Tyler, is this really necessary?" Jacie asked, fumbling into Tyler's front seat, a blindfold around her eyes.

"Trust me, Jacie." Tyler didn't sound like his teasing self. He sounded serious, as if he were God telling her to trust Him. Tyler had been changing lately. The trip to California had done something to him. It wasn't that he had become something different than who he'd always been. It seemed more like he'd grown up. Now he seemed to know when to be funny and when to be serious—rather than making light about nearly everything. He had more levels to him. More sides. It's like his personality had divided into a million pieces, each one fascinating and different.

Jacie slapped Tyler's helping hand. "I can buckle my seatbelt, blindfolded or not."

"Okay, okay," Tyler said. She sensed him backing away. The car door closed, and Tyler went around to the seat next to her. His jacket rustled when he put the key in the ignition. The car shuddered to a start. He made a funny little noise as if he held his breath and the air slowly leaked out through his voice box. She tried to inhale his scent without being obvious. Jessica, his ex-girlfriend, had given him the cologne right before he left for California. The *Brio* gang decided she wanted him to remember he belonged to her. *As if . . .*

Tyler geared the car up, then down. Braking. Slowing to a stop. Starting. Revving. Turning. No more stopping, but lots of curves in the road. More stopping. More starting. No conversation. It was as if, without sight, Jacie could think of little to say. She felt locked in her own mind, a dark closet where she couldn't see anything . . . not even the thoughts stacked around the place. She knew they were there, but couldn't make out their forms. Tyler seemed eager to talk. Something important hovered just behind his silence.

Jacie rummaged around in the dark looking for something to break the awkward quiet. And then she realized Tyler was talking.

". . . I've decided I can trust God in this," he said.

In what? Jacie wondered, having trouble getting out of the dark closet to hear him. She waited, hoping he would say something to give her some idea.

"I know I've been so discouraged."

Jacie nodded.

"I'm beginning to think that often discouragement is just a sign that we don't really believe that God has something better in mind. Ultimately, it's a sign of distrust."

Jacie didn't know what he was referring to. But she feared he might be right.

"I think disappointment is okay," he said. "I mean, we get our hopes up. We expect God to do something particular in our lives, that we and God are thinking the same way about something. Then, *whammo!* It happens. And we're sad and disappointed."

"Like you not getting into CU Boulder," Jacie said.

Tyler was quiet. She hoped he wasn't staring at her like she was nuts, since he probably had just said what the conversation was all about.

Tyler tapped his thumbs against the steering wheel, keeping with the beat of the Dave Matthews tune. "I've been disappointed. Then discouraged."

"Terribly moody," Jacie teased.

"That, too." Tyler gave her shoulder a soft punch. "Sorry about that."

Jacie tipped her head back and laughed. "But your *Brio* girl friends have *never* been moody."

"I'm not going to touch that one."

"Smart boy."

Tyler got serious again. "Really, that's what I'm trying to do: be a smart guy, smarter than before. Not taking the detours in life as though my life is over. Yeah, what I planned for my life may be over. But here's where the trust comes in. And I'm not sure how to do it. I want to trust God. I want to trust that if God has me go to Copper Ridge Community College, He has a reason for that."

Jacie could hear the determination in his voice—mixed with the fear probably of living with his father for another two years. If you could call it living. If you knew that Tyler was already on the edge of losing it with his dad.

As if Tyler could read her mind, he said in a voice attempting not to sound defeated, "I've heard there's a bulletin board at the college. People looking for roommates."

"Aren't you applying elsewhere?" Jacie asked. Her nose tickled. She rubbed it furiously.

"Are you trying to peek?"

"NO!"

Tyler slipped the Dave Matthews CD out and replaced it with one of Jacie's favorites—Dido. He chose it for her, she knew. Not for himself. "I found some schools on the Internet that I've never heard of. All with my major. I've applied to two, and plan to apply to the others as well. Maybe UNC."

"You sound okay with it."

"I am, now. Just trying to trust."

Jacie leaned her head against the window. She felt the tears begin. She was tired of crying. But she didn't know how to stop these days. "I wish I could trust," she said in a soft voice.

Tyler reached over and put his hand on her arm. "Jacie. You're afraid."

"But I don't want to be," she whispered. "I just can't—"

Tyler touched his fingertips to her lips. "It's okay. You will."

"How—"

"I'm not talking about it now. You just have to wait."

"What about Hannah?"

"I can only deal with one of you at a time." Tyler rubbed his hand along his pants. "Besides. As much as she's hurt, I really think God is reaching her. You may need help."

"I'm trying, Tyler."

"I know. But take a little help."

Jacie sighed and leaned her head against the window. She could see Tyler's hand resting on the gear shift beneath the blindfold. He gripped it, then released it. And she knew in her heart . . . Tyler cared an awful lot about *her.* If she ever thought he didn't, she really had been blind. His care for her was suddenly so overwhelming, Jacie thought she'd explode with it.

chapter 18

The car bumped over dirt and gravel, and Dido sang without a warble. Jacie was glad she wasn't prone to carsickness. She would have lost it a long time ago.

The car stopped, the engine cut off. Total silence.

Tyler opened his door into the silence, and still there were no sounds except those Tyler made. He opened her door and helped her out.

Jacie removed her blindfold. She stood in the middle of a moist, blackened place. She turned slowly, taking in all the maimed, brittle trees. "Ty. Why did you bring me here?"

Tyler stood, his hands shoved in his pockets. He didn't say anything. Jacie couldn't read his expression.

"I don't like it."

Tyler nodded.

"It's awful." The desolation and death affected her. She felt it in her gut. In her heart. Behind her eyes. In her throat. She swallowed and blinked in the bright, total destruction of the remnants of a forest fire.

What was that cottony disbelief that choked out real thought? That thick, hazy mist that sat on her mind? This had been a beautiful forest.

She took deeper breaths to stave off tears. She didn't want to sob in front of Tyler. She wished she were at home where she could hide from the ugly feelings.

Tyler moved to touch her. His finger, barely touching her face, moved a curl and tucked it behind her ear. His thumb left a warm stripe down her cheek. He put his arm around her shoulder and pulled her close. "I know," he said.

Jacie tried to look up at him. But he was so close . . .

"Look." Tyler turned her to face the red-tinged stones of Turkey Rock.

All Jacie could see were stones, boulders, and burnt, broken trees, their once upturned branches snapped and hanging, or broken into spiky black twigs that protruded from their blackened trunks. "All I see is death," she said.

Tyler moved his hand to twiddle her curls. "Look deeper."

"I don't get it, Tyler," Jacie said. "What do you want?"

"Look past the death."

Jacie broke free from his side-hug and clomped over to a rock and planted herself on it. She put her elbows on her knees and her chin on her hands. She saw only destruction, and she wasn't sure she *wanted* to see beyond it. The blackened landscape looked an awful lot like how she saw life these days. Ruined. Pointless. Why grow a forest just to destroy it in a matter of hours? And this was just one edge of the thousands of acres of beautiful forest the fire had ripped through, gobbling up all the good, leaving nothing but ugliness behind.

Tyler stood behind her. She leaned back and rested her head against his belly. It happened so naturally, it surprised her.

She didn't know what to do. Stay there? Move away? Good feelings mixed with her anger and hurt. She wanted to ignore what caused the anger and hurt, and melt into the good feelings. But she couldn't. The stark empty forest kept her in reality—a reality where God could not be trusted to do good all the time.

"Why grow a rebellious girl like Dinah into a wonderful woman of God," Tyler offered, "then let disaster rip through and take her and her unborn child?"

Jacie gave an imperceptible nod. Something gnawed at the very core of her being. "What does Pastor Joe say every Sunday?" Jacie said, her voice quiet and soft.

Tyler thought. Pastor Joe had them repeat after him every Sunday. "That God is good—all the time?"

"Yeah." Jacie paused, watching as rock climbers began their ascent up the side of Turkey Rock. "What kind of imaginary world does he live in?"

She could feel Tyler shrug.

"Do you think He is?" she asked.

"God or Pastor Joe?"

Jacie rolled her eyes and sighed.

"Sorry."

"I could give you the old Hannah answer—that God is good, but that doesn't mean we can see everything He does as good."

"I don't want the Hannah answer. I want yours. Do *you* think God is good all the time?"

Tyler took a deep breath, and let it out slowly. "I don't know, Jacie. It doesn't seem like it."

Tears began again. "Then how are we supposed to believe?"

"Believe what, Jacie? The God we've made up in our own imaginations, or the God who really is?" Tyler moved to sit next to her. She scooted a bit to make room for him. He pulled one foot up on the rock and hugged his knee. "We squish God into a tiny box, and when He pops out, we're shocked and horrified. We tell God what He looks like instead of letting God define Himself for us."

"I don't like Him much these days."

"I don't either," Tyler admitted.

"So how come you have any faith left at all?"

He didn't answer.

Jacie let the silence be. She watched the climbers in their slow, deliberate movements sideways and upwards. The multicolored climbing ropes making a zigzag path up the rock. The bodies sometimes stretched to their maximum length, the next move scrunching them to tiny compressed beetles. Each move unlike the last.

Tyler spoke after a long silence. "I guess I believe there are no better options."

Jacie almost gasped. It sounded almost blasphemous. She twisted to look at his face. But he kept his eyes on the rock wall.

"The way I see it," he continued, "I have a few options in this world: Do things my way—trusting myself, a screwed-up human being. Do things the way someone else wants me to—trusting another screwed-up human being. Do things the way the enemy of God would have me do—trusting what I can see. And you know, sometimes that option looks pretty good for a while. My last option, the way I see it, is to do things the way God wants me to—attempting to trust a Being we don't always understand. One who does not always make sense in what He asks or tells me to do."

He picked up Jacie's hand and began to rub her fingers one at a time. "I already know I make a complete mess of things when I'm in charge. I don't trust what others think is right. Yeah, I can create my own god or spirituality the way they do, but really, who am I fooling? I'd still be ultimately following myself. And if I follow some human leader who thinks he has all the answers, I'm just following an arrogant egotist who is more interested in himself than me."

Jacie tried to listen while melting at Tyler's tender touch. She wanted to pay attention to the wonderful feelings flowing from her hand, and wanted to hear what he said. She could move her hand away. But she didn't.

"Like I said, I've seen what the enemy of God does, and it's guaranteed to ultimately lead to some sort of life-sucking horrors. So what does that leave me? A God who is unpredictable, who claims He ultimately does things for our good. But what if that good often comes in a package that looks pretty lousy?"

Jacie thought of Tyler's dad. He claimed to be a Christian but he used his "faith" as a weapon to crush his family. "What if it isn't really good and God is just trying to fool us?"

A climber called to his buddy to show him a handhold. The rope trailed through the carabiners. Jacie thought they looked like colorful geckos.

"I've thought of that. What if God is not *all* good? What then?" Tyler turned to look at her. "Jacie, it ultimately comes back to my options." He shook his head, his blond hair falling into his eyes. He didn't bother to brush it away. "No matter how you look at it, there's only one who stands out as the least bad of all the choices."

Jacie nodded but hated the answer.

Tyler nodded. "It always comes down to a choice of faith, doesn't it? Either we believe God is perfectly good and we trust Him in spite of all the evidence to the contrary. Or we don't believe God is perfectly good, but He's the best option we've got and so we trust that some of what He does will be good."

Jacie frowned. The options she had didn't seem very good. But Tyler had a point. Either way, God was the best choice, and either way, she had to have faith enough to give Him her obedience. Or she'd have to trust herself or someone else equally fallible.

She stared, not really seeing anything. Tyler wisely said nothing.

Her eyes began to focus on something. Yellow—near the ground. And over there. Something purple. "What's that?" she asked, pointing.

Tyler grinned, pushing the hair out of his eyes. "Let's go see," he said. She had no doubt that he already knew what it was. "You really need to get glasses."

She gave him a little punch. "I hate glasses."

They walked through the blackened forest until they came upon the colors. A bright yellow sunflower with a black face turned toward the sun. Bunches of purple statis and tiny brilliant blue flowers—*were they shooting stars?*—gathered, bringing bright color to the darkness.

Jacie looked in awe. "How can they grow here? They're gorgeous." She knelt and caressed them, her fingers a butterfly's touch.

Tyler nodded, crossing his arms.

"Looks like my Jace is beginning to see. You're finally opening your eyes."

Jacie smiled and squeezed her eyes shut.

Tyler poked his finger in her ribs. She yelped, jumped away, and opened her eyes. "Keep them open," he ordered.

She squatted beside the flowers and took them in.

"Common wildflowers," Tyler said. "We see them hiking all the time. Or horseback riding with Sol."

"We do?"

Tyler nodded. "When they're the only thing, they stand out, don't they?"

Jacie stroked them again and stood back, taking in the surroundings. Black against orange-red rock. Purple against ash gray. Blue against orange-red. Yellow-and-black faces following the direction of the sun. Light. Shadow. Life. Death.

"I need to draw," Jacie whispered. "I wish I had brought my things—"

Tyler took off running. He opened the trunk to the car, slammed it shut, and ran back. He plunked Jacie onto a rock and handed her a large sketching tablet.

"Where'd you get this?" She looked up at him. It was a nice pad—expensive paper. "You're so funny."

"Yeah, I'm funny," he said in a serious tone, but with a smirk on his face.

Jacie looked at his hands and flipped back the cover. The paper was thick, beautiful, white—like felt. "Pencils? Chalk?"

Tyler's smirk grew into a full grin. "Nope. What do you see?"

"Tyler." She was growing impatient with his game. If she knew what he expected, she'd spout it off and they could get out of this depressing place. They could get to Becca's early enough for the standard Friday night pizza and movie.

Confused, exasperated, and weary, Jacie exploded. "What do you want from me?" she yelled.

Tyler sighed. "I'm trying to give you something, Jace."

Jacie held the paper in her lap, staring at the white page. This wasn't like Tyler to be so secretive. He was being manipulative. And she hated that.

Tyler didn't say anything. He just sat there, watching the climbers inch their way up the rock.

She moved her hand across the page, and a black smudge trailed behind. She turned her hand over and looked at it. All her fingers had black on them. She looked at her pants. A black smudge marked the side of her knee. She laughed at herself. Tyler laughed too. The beautiful paper soaked up the soot like watercolors. She smudged again. It was an amazing feeling. Her eyes met Tyler's and she looked around. She couldn't walk far without getting black on her.

She stood and walked a few steps to a tree. Some sort of evergreen—or used to be. She peeled off a chunk of burned bark and returned to the rock. She began to draw. The brittle bark broke at times, but it smudged really well. She lost herself in drawing the climbers scaling the rock. She drew the ugly, barren trees rising up. She drew their pitiful, broken branches. Their deformities. The pages flipped as she finished each drawing.

She had no idea how long she sat there drawing. At one point, she looked down, and several colored pencils lay next to her. Sunflower yellow. Cornflower blue. Violet. She turned to smile at Tyler, but he'd gone. She looked around and saw him on another rock, his Bible open in his lap. She'd seen him like that before—at church. At The Edge. Camp. But she couldn't remember ever seeing him on his own.

She drew. It wasn't easy. The thick bark smudged like mad. But she didn't stop.

She drew the color in the midst of the blackness. The life begging to rise out of death.

And then she saw.

chapter 19

Jacie left the sketchbook, bark charcoal, and pencils. She quietly walked to stand in front of Tyler. He shaded his eyes as he looked up from the Bible at her.

"I know why you brought me here," she said, feeling those stupid tears hunkering down in her chest again, wanting to burst forth and humiliate her.

Tyler closed his Bible. He raised his eyebrow.

She sat next to him and pointed. "Life," she said. "Look at it. Insistent. Determined. Life out of disaster. Good things out of bad. It's almost as if you can't stop the flowers from coming."

Tyler said nothing, but a smile tugged at the corner of his mouth.

"I started looking around. And you know? The flowers are coming up all over the place. Not just in that one little spot."

Jacie hugged her knees to her chest, getting black soot all over her. She didn't care. "I wish I could explain how I feel.

What I see. But I can't." She looked at Tyler, desperate for him to understand. Because if he could understand, maybe she could, too. "Something is shifting inside. Like an incredible insight that's perched on the edge of my brain. But it's not quite through."

Tyler ruffled her hair, his smile full. "You're getting it."

"So tell me! Finish it for me!"

"I can't," he said. "You have to let your own heart tell you what it is."

"You sound like an old movie. You know, the one that says you have to figure out what's most important to you?"

"*City Slickers*. Funny flick. But, yeah. It's kind of like that, I guess. Only I could probably help you sort it out. I want you to see it yourself. I want you to understand it yourself." He tugged at his ear. "No one can make you trust God, Jace. I have enough trouble with that on my own. I don't have the energy to change something that big." He looked at the huge rock in front of them. "And I can't be God for you. I can't explain things to you the way He can. I just wanted to give you the opportunity to see what I discovered here."

"Trust."

Tyler shrugged. "Yes and no."

"That life is more powerful than death?"

"Cliché. But sort of."

Jacie felt some of the darkness inside dimming as if a distant light were making it gray instead of black. "I'm going to go draw some more."

Tyler nodded. "Between drawing and letting God work inside your thick skull, I think you'll get it."

"Wow, thanks, Ty. You're a real encourager."

"Hey. It's my gift."

She slugged him, then went back to her drawing things.

She sat and looked for a long time. She drew. She sat. And then she was done. At least for now.

Tyler must have realized it and shuffled on over. "You finished? We should head back pretty soon."

"Okay." She ripped a clean piece of paper out of her book. She went to various trees, and took the most burned pieces of wood from them. She gathered some from the ground and wrapped them inside the paper.

"What are you doing?" Tyler asked.

"Taking some of the lesson home with me."

Tyler pointed up at the rock. "Look. They made it."

Jacie looked at the climbers sitting on the top, resting from their hard work. "That's us, isn't it?" she asked Tyler.

He looked at her, then let his gaze follow where she pointed. He said nothing.

"The *Brio* gang is like a group of climbers. We're tied to the same rock of school and friends and Copper Ridge. We've been climbing together for a long time with Solana and Becca. Hannah's come along to join us. We each take turns being in the lead. And we each take turns being the anchor. When one falls, they don't fall far because someone is there to catch them."

Jacie felt something odd nearly overtake her. She wanted to kiss Tyler so bad. Just a thank-you kiss, of course. She had to blink and turn away. Tyler moved next to her and rested his hand on her shoulder. She leaned against his chest. "Thanks, Ty, for being my anchor today. I've been falling—too far."

"I know," Tyler whispered. "You've been scaring me."

Jacie held still. "Really?" she whispered back.

He reached into the back pocket of his jeans and pulled out a 3 x 5 card folded in half. "Here," he said, handing it to her.

Jacie opened it and read, "Oh LORD, be thou to me a rock of habitation to which I may continually come. Psalm 71:3."

She looked at it, letting the words soak in. She looked up at Turkey Rock, then back at the card. *That's what I need. It's what I want. A rock. Something solid, unmovable. Something I cannot change. But is that really God?*

She folded the card and handed it back to him. "Thanks," she said softly.

"I don't want you to lose your faith, Jace." His arm squeezed her tightly against him. "I want you to see beyond the burned forest. I want you to see the zigzag route to the top of the rock wall. Nothing is straightforward in this world. Nothing is as easy as it looks. So many things are more confusing than understandable."

"Dang, Ty. You sound like a youth leader."

Tyler let go of her. He dropped his hand into his pocket and retrieved his keys. "Let's go."

Jacie felt fear zip through her. What had she said wrong?

Tyler opened the car door for her and waited for her to get in and situate her bundle of bark and sketch pad before he closed the door. He entered the car on his side and stuck the keys in the ignition, turning the engine over. The car bumped over some rough spots, then leveled onto the maintained dirt-and-gravel road. Dido sang until Tyler turned her off.

"Jacie, California did something to me."

Jacie looked at him, but said nothing. She was afraid of saying or doing the wrong thing.

"I told you guys some of what happened, but not all of it. Out there, I learned that the line between right and wrong is sometimes blurred, that we have to look beyond what is obvious to find truth and right. Or what God wants. Sure, you have groups that are blatantly blasphemous, or endorsing sex that is far from what God would say is pure. But there are also people and songs and life that contain some truth. Sometimes far more truth than lies. Unraveling which is which isn't always easy."

He took a deep breath. "So, if I sound like a youth leader, maybe it's because Allen and I have been talking these things through so much lately. I don't necessarily always believe exactly as he does. But together we're exploring this world where the lie is told that we can make up what's right for ourselves, and that's perfectly okay, that defining my reality by my reality is all that anyone requires. Society seems to have no absolutes anymore."

"I know," Jacie said. "And even God doesn't seem to have absolutes."

Tyler nodded. "Yeah! I mean, Jace, I don't want you to lose your faith, but I also don't want it to be a false faith. I think Hannah's great—" Tyler's cheeks flushed, probably at remembering his mistaken kiss at the ski lodge. "But I also felt like her faith wasn't based on anything really solid."

"She was parroting what her family taught her," Jacie said kindly.

"Right. But now that something has happened outside of her pat-answer zone, it's blown her up."

"Yes and no," Jacie said, thinking about some of their talks of late. "She's struggling—"

"I mean, the faith that wasn't solid blew up, not the faith that is real. What was real is left and continues to grow. It's going to get her through this."

"Ahh."

"So now that her faith has a chance to become solid and so incredibly real, nothing is going to stop that girl."

Jacie sat silent. Tyler was right. Hannah was a fireball about faith before, but now, it was going to be coming from a different place that would make all her zeal real, rather than surface. It had already begun.

"The point is, Jacie, that if you can see beyond the fire zone, maybe God will have a chance to show you the flowers that are growing in spite of the destruction. Maybe your faith will also grow more solid."

"I don't know, Ty. I'm still pretty scared of God. I don't want to get wiped out before I'm 30. If He's going to do that, I might as well do everything I want to do."

"What if He doesn't?" Tyler asked. "Would you be sorry that you hadn't lived life His way? That you hadn't trusted the wonderful things that He might do in your life?"

Jacie sighed, her heart grasping for something that would make Tyler understand her fear, what she saw and felt. "Look at my mom! What kind of wonderful things does she have? God hasn't made her life any easier. She has nothing great as a result of trusting God."

"She has you."

"Like that's some great prize."

Tyler pulled over to the side of the road so abruptly that it frightened Jacie. He threw the gear into park and took her cheeks into his hands. "Listen to me, Jacie. You are the biggest prize any guy could ever hope for."

Jacie felt awash with discomfort, as if what he said had to be a lie. She tried to turn away from his grip, his gaze.

Tyler turned her face again toward his. "You are the most wonderful girl I've ever known. I'm just sorry that it took me so long to admit it to myself."

Jacie felt hamsters running on a wheel in her stomach.

"No one is as authentic as you. . . ."

"Except Solana?" Jacie asked, hoping her teasing would divert this uncomfortable place.

"You're right. Solana and Becca and Hannah are all authentic," Tyler said. "But none of them has your heart, your compassion, your depth of spirit. None of them has a faith that is real enough to challenge God. Jacie. They aren't like you. No one is like you."

Jacie tried to nod, but couldn't with his grip on her cheeks. He must have realized how hard he held her cheeks and loosened his grip. He started to stroke her cheeks with his thumbs.

"No one is like me," Jacie said, "because I'm so weird. Funny-looking. Quirky."

"All the reasons why I—" Tyler opened his mouth to finish his sentence and then stopped.

The way he looked at her, Jacie thought she would melt. She thought he would kiss her. Did she want him to? She did, and she didn't. She didn't want him to because that would make her think he liked her. And although she realized that's what she wanted, she knew he didn't really like her in that way. She looked away.

Tyler dropped his hands and shifted into gear. The car pulled away from the side of the street. "Just don't ever, ever, forget how special you are, Jace, and how being different from everyone else is, in your case, a very good thing. Anyone who knows you, who is fortunate enough to spend time with you, knows they are very lucky."

Jacie stared out the side window at the trees going by, her mind cluttered with all the information thrown at her today. *God, help me sort it out*, she prayed. *Help me find You again.*

chapter 20

Tyler stopped the car outside the elementary school grounds. Without a word he opened her door, took her hand, and held it all the way to Alyeria. He let go so she could duck through the shrubs first.

Jacie perched herself on the edge of a log. She leaned forward, letting her arms fall between her legs. "Thanks, Ty." She felt the tears in her heart, wanting to express themselves.

Tyler shrugged. He knelt in front of her. He looked at the ground, then up at her. He took a deep breath. "Do you want me to leave?"

Jacie shook her head. She wanted him here in case God showed up and scared her to death.

"Do you need to talk to God alone?"

Jacie bit her bottom lip. "I don't know what to say."

"The truth."

"That I choose Him?"

Tyler nodded.

"In spite of the fact that I don't fully trust Him yet?"

Tyler nodded again.

Jacie sighed. "Don't you think that makes Him mad? That He wants all our trust or nothing?"

Tyler laughed. "If that were true, I think God would be mad at everybody. Nobody totally trusts God, Jace."

Jacie rocked back and forth, considering.

"Allen says God is more concerned about relationship."

"What does that *mean*?" Jacie asked. "I hear that all the time, but I don't understand it."

Tyler sat on the log next to Jacie and took her hand. "You and I have a relationship. We talk. We share things. You share things with the other *Brio* friends. We tell each other what we're thinking. We ask questions. We wonder together. We call each other up the moment something newsworthy happens. We drop everything to go be with the others when something big happens. We care about each other. That's a relationship."

Jacie considered even more.

"We get mad at each other, but that doesn't mean we aren't friends anymore. We tell each other that we're mad, we talk about it, forgive, and get over it. Our relationship is actually stronger when we go through lots of stuff—good and bad—together. It's not always good. If it was, I don't think we'd have such great friendships."

Tears started to pour down Jacie's face. She wrapped her arms around her waist and began to cry—really cry. "Is it okay, God, if we just talk? Is it okay if I tell You I'm mad? Is it okay that I want to trust You and don't want to trust You and can't trust You all at the same time? Because I really don't like life without You."

A soft breeze blew through the aspens, rustling their leaves, and through her, rustling her doubts.

She looked at Tyler and swiped at her tears. "It's okay, isn't it?"

Tyler nodded and gave her a soft smile. The breeze lifted his blond hair and set it down in a different style. He cupped her chin in his hand and rubbed his thumb across her cheek. He leaned forward.

When his soft lips touched hers, tears began to flow again. She put her arms around his neck and kissed him back.

When Tyler ended the kiss, he looked at her, his eyes searching hers. "You know that I love you, don't you?"

Jacie looked away. "Well, of course."

Tyler took her chin and turned her to look at him. "No, Jace. Not like that . . . I *love you.*"

Jacie couldn't find words in her head. Where had they all gone?

"I've been stupid for many years. But maybe I needed to be. I suppose that was best."

Jacie looked at him, confused by his babbling.

"I mean, I've overlooked the best girl in my life. But I think that we've tried and tested our friendship. We never played games to impress the other. So now we know the real character of the other."

She smiled and played with his fingers.

"I would love for you to consider thinking about me as more than a friend." He raised his eyebrows.

The voice inside Jacie sang, "At last!" She wanted to dive into the joy and warmth and belonging, but her practical side stood up and took charge. "We have college," she said.

"Yeah. And we'll probably be terribly mature and not confine ourselves to each other if we're not at the same school—which we probably won't be. But I'd like for you to still consider keeping me in mind, and I'll be keeping you in mind."

Jacie tried not to laugh. He was so cute right now—stumbling over thoughts and words. Still, her heart raced as she put together words she wanted to say. "Tyler, I do love you very much. I love how you've grown up—especially since California. I love who you are becoming. "I'd like to continue growing what we have and if nothing else, to always be friends."

"That's all I ask," Tyler said, pulling her close and giving her a hug that she suddenly realized she'd always wanted from him.

● ● ●

Black covered everything. Faces, arms, fingers, clothes, paper.

"Smudge!" Jacie said. "Smudge for gray, color for black. Think about death! Think about light. Think about rebirth. Re-growth. Think about how you feel when you feel hurt. Then think about how you feel when light comes in. Make different pictures."

Her students scraped bark across white paper and smudged away. Brenda drew stark lines and smudged flowers from them. Most of her students smiled for the first time ever in her class. Nora chatted with Marlene, tucking blackened bark into her strap and taking it out again, occasionally guiding Marlene's waving arm a little closer to the paper.

Mrs. R appeared at the door, clipboard in hand. "Jacie, I need to talk with you," she said.

Jacie stepped into the hallway with her. Mrs. R took a deep breath. She tapped the clipboard with the pen. "Jacie, I'm not sure this is working out."

Jacie felt something drop inside—some piece of her perhaps. "What do you mean?"

She looked at her clipboard and then at Jacie. "It seems the students are frustrated that they aren't learning anything."

Jacie nodded. "I'm not a very good teacher."

Mrs. R took a deep breath. "I don't know why they keep coming back if they're so dissatisfied. I guess they keep hoping—"

"Mrs. Robeson, it's okay. I've felt frustrated that I don't

seem to be able to teach them anything." Her heart felt sick. A failure. *Again*. She bit her bottom lip, hoping she wouldn't cry.

Mrs. R put up her hand to silence her. "What I think, Jacie, is that not everyone can teach. There's no shame in that. You are a wonderful artist and that's why I chose you. The fact that you haven't yet learned how to teach others what you do naturally is okay."

Jacie opened her mouth, but Mrs. R put her hand up again.

"I suggest that if you wish to continue to bring in art supplies and supervise, we'll have art play day instead. No expectations except they can use what you bring."

Jacie didn't know what to do. How to think fast enough. She wanted to just quit. Why continue to remind herself that she'd failed at teaching and now all she had to do was bring stuff and supervise? But then, she saw Marlene and Nora—a friendship and teamwork that didn't really matter if they did anything worthwhile. And Ricky's success with clay. And that for an hour once a week Brenda and some of the other adults could put their hurts and thoughts into something other than their dismal financial situations.

"Okay, Mrs. Robeson."

Mrs. Robeson gave her clipboard a definitive tap. "Okay. That will do fine." She spun on her heels and walked away.

Jacie opened the door and stepped into a new role.

● ● ●

School seems to be on a greased skid headed toward graduation. The speed at which I will be a quasi-adult scares me and has been causing annoying reflection in me.

Grace and Mom are together constantly. Mom has taken her to obedience school. Now they do everything together. I feel left out. I thought kids were supposed to pull away from their parents. Instead, my mom is pulling away from me. She's getting a lot of phone calls that she's taking in her room rather than roaming around the house with the cordless like she usually does. I'd love to eavesdrop. But the moment I do, Grace sneaks up onto the sofa for a comfy snooze. I swear she and Mom have this all planned. I also think "OFF!" is the most frequently said word in the house. So what about obedience training for sofas?

I guess I have to realize that Mom is trying to create a comfortable life before I leave. So that she's not as lonely as some of her friends have been when their kids have gone to college. I guess I should allow her that. But honestly, I want her all to myself. I want her to always be available when I need her. The fact that she might not be scares me to death.

I try not to think about Dad not coming for graduation. Sometimes I'm great at denial, and sometimes I'm not. Whatever, he's not coming and I have to deal with it.

Becca is less sad as the days go by. She and Nate e-mail a hundred times a day. They plan to go to the same university if they can swing it. Their choices are narrowing and the possibilities of that happening look really good.

Solana and Becca get together for crying

parties over their lost boys. But Sol is becoming increasingly excited about UC Berkeley. Her work at the Greenhouse is paying off and her boss, Ellie, said she might be able to transfer to a similar conservancy in California.

Hannah. Wow. What can I say about Hannah? The girl who used to be so obnoxious with her pat answers has become the most amazing, compassionate Christian I've ever met. I used to wish she'd go away. Now I can't be around her enough. We talk about Dinah and God and life and trust and the uncertainty of everything—and how that is something we have to embrace and take into ourselves as part of trusting God. She is so good to talk with now.

Tyler has been accepted to University of Northern Colorado. He'll get the pre-reqs out of the way, then try to transfer to Boulder. He'll be away from his father and still have a chance for his dream. I'll miss him terribly while I'm at school in San Francisco. But there's always e-mail. And there's always hope that God will direct everything we do so that we don't have to stress about whether or not we'll have a future together or apart. What's important now is to just enjoy being together and encouraging each other to ask good questions about God and trust God will answer them.

Ooops—there's the doorbell. Gotta run. It might be Nora.

chapter 21

The *Brios* looked like choir members circled together in their black graduation robes.

"We want to pray for Jacie's speech," Hannah said to Solana.

"So?" Solana said, her voice trying to be snotty but failing.

Jacie looked at her. She could see something was shifting inside Solana. Something big. But certainly something she would deny. "Sol. Please pray with us this time," Jacie said, reaching out her hand.

Solana gave a big sigh. A fake one, Jacie decided. Solana took Jacie's hand. "If you're forcing me to."

"I am," Jacie said gently to save Solana's secret. But she could tell the others knew what she did—that Solana really did want to pray with them.

"Help Jacie not to be afraid," Becca said.

"And to be confident that You will use her words in ways

she'll never expect—and might never know about," Hannah said.

Tyler squeezed Jacie's hand as he spoke. "Give my girl the ability to let loose the personality that You gave her. I know You want to use her—all of us—just as we are. Now. And every day to come."

Jacie wasn't surprised when Solana spoke next. In that flash a few moments ago she knew she wouldn't have to worry about Solana anymore. Her day was coming. Maybe still a few years down the road. But she was on her way. A tear traveled down Jacie's cheek.

"Hey, God. I suppose You're listening to these guys. So I don't really know if I should talk or not. But everyone here seems to need You in some way. I hope You think about that and don't let us—I mean, them—down."

Jacie held back rivers of tears. She could hardly talk. But she wanted to. "God. It's not fair to ask anything of You since I've been mad at You. But I want to thank You for not giving up on me, even when I wanted to give up on You. I honestly don't care what happens out there as long as You'll let me step back inside Your circle again. And if my words can actually make any one person think differently about You, that would be worth it."

"Line up!" The call came from the cavernous underbelly of the arena. "Ten minutes until the march."

The friends looked at each other. Becca swiped under her eyes. Solana stood straight and blinked a lot. Hannah let tears roll down her face. Tyler swallowed hard. Then, without speaking, they wrapped their arms around each other in a solid group hug. The words "I love you guys" lived in Jacie's heart, but couldn't come out. As they backed up from the hug, she could see the words coming from all of them. Silent and strong. Unspoken, yet shouted.

Jacie moved toward the front of the line where she would

march in with all the dignitaries. She stood in her place behind the senior class president and the valedictorian. She clutched the stack of 3 x 5 cards in her hand.

But she didn't think about the speech. Instead, little movies played quickly in her mind: The day they let Tyler into Alyeria. The day they made the pact. The day Becca broke her arm trying to climb a tree to save a cat. The memories came quickly. Some as photographs. Some as short films. In all of them she saw what she had only taken for granted before. Faithful friends. Fighting. Caring. Supporting. Criticizing. Their bond growing with the years.

It didn't matter what would happen on stage. Even if she bombed big time, they would love her. Her mother would love her. God would love her. If God could love her even when she was furious at Him, when she accused Him of being cold-hearted and cruel, when she didn't trust Him . . . If He could love her even when she couldn't see Him beyond her own fears and desires, then it didn't matter what others thought about her. It didn't matter what the crowd thought. Certain people loved her. *Always.*

"Pomp and Circumstance" began, leading them forward into the arena. It was the same song that had led so many other graduates to a place of ending, yet opening the door to something new—a new world, life from death.

Jacie didn't hear the announcements. She sat on the folding chair trying to keep herself sitting properly and not doing any of her nervous habits—like swinging her leg or letting her foot joggle up and down so it looked like her leg had a nervous habit of its own.

She stood for the national anthem. She sat while the school district's superintendent gave a speech. The band played a song. And then she heard her name. She took five steps from her folding chair on the stage to the podium. As she stepped up to it, the senior class president put a square platform of wood down. Jacie blushed and stood on the platform so she didn't look lost behind the giant podium.

She hoped she wouldn't throw up. Or wet her pants. Her insides trembled. She took a deep breath. She scanned the audience. She thought she might pass out. But as she shifted her gaze to her notes, she had to see the audience at the foot of the stage—her classmates and her *Brio* friends. The beloved group that began in elementary school. The friendship that time and distance would not destroy.

"Good morning, seniors! Can you believe it? We're finally here!"

At that moment, all fear left. She didn't care if she messed up. She didn't care if people liked her speech. It didn't matter anymore. She had what mattered.

"For many of us, next year will be the first time on our own, the first time in a new place, and for some, the first time away from friends and family who have been there forever. It will be scary, and different, but we must use this chance to see, do, and be.

"We've all had firsts in our lives: the first day of school, the first bike ride, the first roller coaster adventure. Each first loomed ahead as an extraordinary feat to be conquered. Now, we can look back and see how much we've learned from each situation and how we've been blessed by each new experience. We must continue to learn to take chances and to overcome the obstacles that are thrown our way.

"The great inventor of the Model T, Henry Ford, once said, 'Obstacles are those *frightful* things you see when you take your eyes off the goal.'

"So, as we journey on in future years, let us continue to set goals and challenges for ourselves. It is okay to look back on what we've had or experienced in the past, but let's never forget to look forward. Keep your eyes on the prize, go for what you want, and don't let the fear of change stop you. Ask yourself, 'What would you *do* if you weren't *afraid*?'

"So, don't look at the future wondering how or why, but wonder, 'Why not?'

"We've had great times together, shared great memories, and have even shared great pain. As we continue on, let us not forget the friends, family members, and teachers who have taught us so much and have guided us through these times. Instead, may we see the wings they have helped us to grow to *soar* through the future.

"Recently I took a trip to where the forest fires ravaged our mountains this past summer. I was horrified at the bleak, black devastation." She looked at Tyler, who grinned at her.

"But once I paid attention, I saw that already wildflowers were beginning to grow.

"Fellow classmates," she said, leaning over the podium to scan the seniors seated before her, "I promise that you will have events in your life that will burn down your forest—your dreams, your ideals of the perfect life."

She looked directly at Hannah. Then Becca. Then Solana. Then Tyler. Each of them had experienced just such losses.

"But if you wait. If you trust. If you look for it, you will see new life. And not just any life. But *wild*flowers. Something wild. Something beautiful. Something with new colors. A wild beauty.

"Don't be afraid of it. Be excited. For the new growth is something you may not ever be able to imagine. But it gives hope. It lets you know that death is never the end. There is always new life . . . if you only know where to look for it."

FOCUS ON THE FAMILY®

Welcome to the Family!

Whether you received this book as a gift, borrowed it, or purchased it yourself, we're glad you read it. It's just one of the many helpful, insightful, and encouraging resources produced by Focus on the Family.

In fact, that's what Focus on the Family is all about — providing inspiration, information, and biblically based advice to people in all stages of life.

It began in 1977 with the vision of one man, Dr. James Dobson, a licensed psychologist and author of 18 best-selling books on marriage, parenting, and family. Alarmed by the societal, political, and economic pressures that were threatening the existence of the American family, Dr. Dobson founded Focus on the Family with one employee and a once-a-week radio broadcast aired on only 36 stations.

Now an international organization, the ministry is dedicated to preserving Judeo-Christian values and strengthening and encouraging families through the life-changing message of Jesus Christ. Focus ministries reach families worldwide through 10 separate radio broadcasts, two television news features, 13 publications, 18 Web sites, and a steady series of books and award-winning films and videos for people of all ages and interests.

• • •

For more information about the ministry, or if we can be of help to your family, simply write to Focus on the Family, Colorado Springs, CO 80995 or call (800) A-FAMILY (232-6459). Friends in Canada may write Focus on the Family, PO Box 9800, Stn Terminal, Vancouver, BC V6B 4G3 or call (800) 661-9800. Visit our Web site — www.family.org — to learn more about Focus on the Family or to find out if there is an associate office in your country.

We'd love to hear from you!

Want More? Life
Go from ordinary to extraordinary! *Want More? Life* will help you open the door to God's abundant life. You'll go deeper, wider and higher in your walk with God in the midst of everyday challenges like self-image, guys, friendships and big decisions. Spiral hardcover.

Want More? Love
You may ask, "Does God really love me? How can He love me — with all my faults and flaws?" *Want More? Love* is a powerful devotional that shows you how passionately and protectively God loves and cares for you — and how you can love Him in return! Spiral hardcover.

Bloom: A Girl's Guide to Growing Up

You have lots of questions about life. In *Bloom: A Girl's Guide To Growing Up*, your questions are addressed and answered with the honesty youth expect and demand. From changing bodies, to dating and sex, to relationships, money and more, girls will find the answers they need. Paperback.

Brio

It's the inside scoop — with hot tips on everything from fashion and fitness to real-life faith. Monthly magazine.

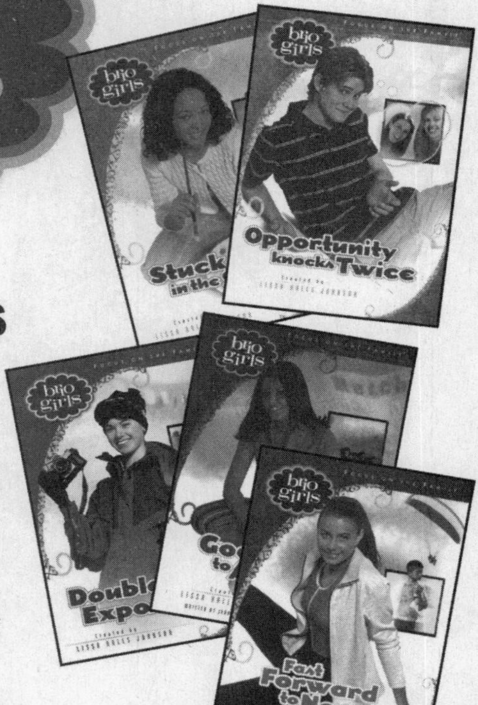

Real Faith Meets Real Life℠

Five friends. Five views of God. Five ways of dealing with life. The *Brio Girls®* series follows Jacie, Becca, Hannah, Tyler and Solana through a variety of circumstances that challenge their faith and their friendships. Join them as they share their painful, funny, and revealing stories.

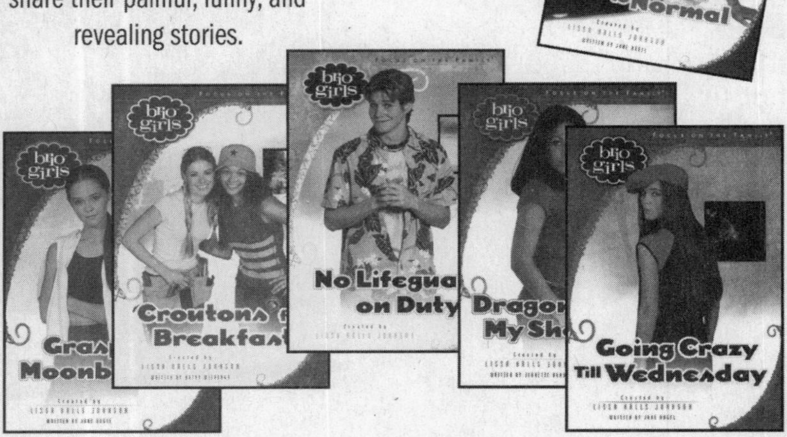